To
Wilma

Enjoy in Christ

Kenneth L Clark
6-30-02

The Adventures In Nit Picky

Home of the Fighting Tomcats

by
Kenneth L. Clark

Library of Congress Control Number: 2002091950

ISBN 0-9720043-0-0

First printing –1000 copies - May, 2002

Printed in the USA by
Morris Publishing
3212 East Highway 30
Kearney, NE 68847
1-800-650-7888

Contents

Contents (continued)

Foreword

Throughout human history, storytelling has played an integral part of the human life experience. As children, we are told stories to entertain us, to teach us, and to mature us. No matter our age, we all enjoy hearing a good story or even telling a good story. Many times the stories we hear triggers one of our own counter-stories, about a time and event in our past. *The Adventures In Nit Picky* is a collection of stories that take you back to those simple days of one's own childhood. When reading the stories, you will find yourself laughing, crying, remembering your past, and stopping to reflect on your own life and what is really important.

I always teach that the most important word in the English language is the word "RELATIONSHIP". Without relationship with God and others, we cannot experience life to it's fullest. Ken Clark, through his masterful stories, reminds us how relationships should be valued and how we should treat others. The stories are told with a Biblical based truth to every story.

Ken Clark is a gifted storyteller. This in itself is what helps the "Nit Picky" stories come to life. But the real reason that these stories are so stirring is that Ken is a godly man that knows how to treat others. Ken is a friend that values the relationships that God has placed in his path.

The Adventures In Nit Picky is a book that will be loved by all, no matter one's age. It is one of those books that has something for everyone, that you will read over and over again and will want to share with others.

Greg Doussard

Gregory a. Doussard

Acknowledgments

With special thanks to:
My wife, Mary Sue, and friends Jeanette Fuller, Joyce
Cooksey, Greg Doussard, and Cindy Workman for their
suggestions and long hours of proof reading.
Thanks also to my family, friends, and church families
of Jerome Lane Baptist Church, Cahokia, IL. and First
Southern Baptist Church, South Roxana, IL. for their
love, patience, support, and encouragement to write
these stories into book form.

A GOOD PAST MAKES FOR A BETTER
TOMORROW

Dedication

**I dedicate this book with sincere love, fond
memories, and deep gratitude to all
my family, teachers, and friends
who nurtured me through my growing up days
in Mounds, Illinois.**

Welcome to the Town
of Nit Picky

    Whether you are growing up or grew up in a large city, a small town, or on the back roads of America, it really doesn't matter when it comes to these stories. The lessons to be learned in the little town of Nit Picky, home of the Fighting Tomcats, are of value to all.

    To appreciate more fully these adventures of the Nit Picky kids, please step back in time with me, the "Aged Storyteller", and visit our town. Oh yes, the town of Nit Picky and its characters are fictitious all right; but they're recognizable and believable. Probably every one of you have met or seen many of our town's folks and places. But take a moment and journey with me as we quickly tour the streets of Nit Picky.

    It's a place of 1800 people or so and who knows how many cats and dogs. Nit Picky is nestled at the base of a small ridge of hills to the north and is bordered some miles to the east and west by large rivers. Like many small towns, it once was a booming metropolis. Railroads were big at one time, causing the town to have two banks. However by the Fifties and Sixties, the time of these stories, those prosperous days were past. All that remains now of the large railroad yards are their spooky foundations hidden in the entangled brush west of the tracks. The town's aged train station, scarred from disuse, sits forlornly by the rails. Across from the station and halfway up Rail Street stands the ghostly marble columns of the Second National Bank. Both the station and the bank are boarded-up reminders of Nit Picky's past glory.

An important fact to remember in this visit is that the town's grade school consists of eight grades and its high school has freshmen through seniors. That information will come in handy later. The town has several small businesses, including a dry-goods shop or two, a drug store, and a Five and Dime Emporium. A Piggly Wiggly food market, three or so taverns, several churches, and a doctor's office or two also line Nit Picky's streets. There is one or sometimes two barber poles rotating their stripes on Main Street. A mossy wood-slatted tower stands by the old icehouse splashing water down its sides like a huge waterfall. Besides cooling the ice, its mist cools the kids in the hot summer. Many folks still use the block ice to chill food in their iceboxes. The coal yard is behind the icehouse. Some folks burn coal in potbelly stoves to heat their houses.

The town also has a movie theater called the Roxie. With its quarter matinees, nickel popcorn, soda, and Juicy Fruit candies, the kids spend many a Saturday afternoon giggling at the older teens making out in the back rows. The movie house is popular with the Nit Picky gang because televisions are scarce, and in black and white. Many of the movies, however, are in Technicolor. *Tarzan* and *Maw and Paw Kettle* are popular on the "big screen".

The southwest corner of Main and Third streets is home to Max's Corner Drug Store. The grade school kids peer in its windows with envious eyes as the high school bunch gather for their after-school cherry Cokes, root beer floats, and music from the jukebox. Down the street a few blocks is a small tile building that houses Sam Goodson's Service Station. Sam is the type that

2

always takes the time to air up a kid's bicycle tire. He washes your car's windshield and checks its oil level and tires' air pressure. As he fills your gas tank, he'll catch you up with the latest town "news". Although his hands are rough from hard work and black from grease, and his cap forever smudged with oil, Sam's face wears a perpetual smile. His heart beats with kindness for all needing his assistance.

Next to Sam's place is a little brown-sided store known as Charlie's Market. It is a mom-and-pop grocery store with home delivery for both the elderly and the lazy. It's a kid-friendly store where baseball cards, sherbet pushups, Popsicles, and penny-candy are in great supply. Across from Charlie's we see the local hamburger hangout called the "What-A-Burger". The burgers, true to name, are so large that it normally takes two of the Nit Picky troop to devour one, that is with the exception of "Clutts" Clinkmyer who you'll meet a bit later.

Another place to remember is located several blocks across town from Charlie's and two blocks due north of the Nit Picky Grade School. It is the cemetery hill that stretches high above the town and its creek that flows at the hill's base. That hill, known by the kids as "THE HILL," is home to most of Nit Picky's dead folks. No doubt you'll hear about this place again. It's from atop this lofty ridge overlooking the Nit Picky Grade School that I, the "Aged Storyteller", sit by an etched stone and remember the following childhood adventures.

NIT PICKY GRADE SCHOOL

3

Chapter

1   New Kid in Town

On the first day that Franny attended the Nit Picky Grade School, home of the Fighting Tomcats, Phil laughed at her. Franny heard and knew that she was the object of his amusement. It was happening again; she knew it would.

Franny Goodman was different from the rest of the children, especially this boy known to all of the kids as "Perfect," "Perfect" Phil. Franny had a speech problem that gave her a lisp when she talked. Her large eyeglasses were as thick as the bottom of a Coca-Cola bottle. They made her blue eyes appear as huge as silver dollars. Her light-brown hair was frizzled and lacked luster. She was a wisp of child, pale in color. Franny walked with a pronounced limp and if all of that were not enough, she also had a scar on her neck.

"'Flawed' Franny," joked Phil to the rest of the gang, "that's what we'll call her."

The kids laughed, as kids sometimes do. Again Franny heard, but this time with a trace of tears behind those saucer-sized glasses. Many children in Franny's situation would have felt hate for her hecklers; Franny, however, just felt sadness. She had learned to accept her condition, so would they.

Now, "Perfect" Phil was a nice enough fellow all right, but he was stuck on himself. He was quite talented and smart, usually making A's on all his papers. He took pleasure on being a "pet" of most of his teachers. Phil was also quite proud of his natural ability to play the trumpet. Unlike most children his age, he loved to show off his musical skills when his folks had company or when the school or church had special programs.

When Phil could not find anyone else to listen to his horn, he'd entertain Tiny, his St. Bernard dog. Tiny would never fail to cock his huge head toward the sky, release a deep, agonizing howl, and then dash into the dog house placing his front paws over his ears. Once, Tiny even bolted over the fence and didn't return home for three days. Undaunted, Phil thought to himself, "There will always be critics, besides, what do dogs know about great music anyhow?"

As you might suspect, "Perfect" Phil had become quite puffed up. He even asked his folks to install a larger mirror in his room so that he could truly admire his charm. Unlike most of his grade school buddies, Phil was forever primping his hair, shoes, and clothes.

Thinking himself superior, Phil didn't like to associate with others who didn't fit his perfect world. He would try to avoid being seen anywhere near kids like "Flawed" Franny. That is until that fateful Friday.

Phil had decided that since he was so smart in shop class, he'd sneak in after school and finish his project ahead of the other boys. He reasoned that he really didn't need teacher Hammersmith around to supervise him. But when the slow turning machine caught his apron string and pulled him toward a very painful injury, he thought otherwise.

"HELP!" cried the not-so-perfect Phil. "SAVE ME!" he yelled. His snagged apron tugged him away from the off-switch.

Because of the teasing that Phil and the gang had hurled at Franny, she usually waited to leave school for her four-block walk home. That Friday afternoon was no different. She had stayed late to help Mrs. Playwright straighten up her English room. "Flawed" Franny, with all her physical imperfections, did have something quite special that "Perfect" Phil and the others had missed. She had a generous heart that was filled with Christ's love, kindness, and forgiveness.

Finishing her good deed, Franny made her way down the long, vacated hallway and out of the building. Passing the shop, which was off to itself at the back of the school, she heard Phil's screams. Franny rushed into the shop to see Phil being pulled within inches of the rotating cylinder. Even with her limp,

5

Franny was able to move faster than was ever imagined possible by Phil and the rest of the Nit Picky kids.

Phil's fear had become such a disabling panic that he couldn't tell Franny what to do. Looking around, she saw the power switch. With a quick snap she shut off the machine. It had not been a minute too soon either, for Phil's perfect face was near to losing its perfection.

"G-e-e, t-h-a-n-k-s, Franny," Phil slowly stuttered.

Not wanting a girl, especially Franny, to see his fear and embarrassment, Phil wouldn't look up. He held to the machine tightly for support as he managed to escape his entanglement. Franny, seeing that Phil would be okay, slipped out quietly and went home. She never mentioned that fearful day to Phil again, nor did she ever tell another soul about his mishap.

That night in his room, Phil read his Bible and prayed. People sometimes do that when they're scared and Phil had truly been scared that day. One verse no doubt that the Lord led him to was Ephesians 4:2 where the Bible says: "Be completely humble and gentle; be patient, bearing with one another in love."

Phil wept to himself in front of his large mirror, which mockingly reflected the person he had become. He wept at what he saw and at how he had mistreated others, especially Franny. Phil realized that he too was flawed and vowed that, with Jesus' help, he would start to look beyond the flaws of others. He kept that vow and became one of the best friends Franny ever had. No one laughed at Franny again, at least within Phil's hearing.

And the project he was working on that day in shop, well, he finally did finish it with the help of Mr. Hammersmith. Phil kept it for years as a continual reminder of the day his life changed for the better.

Chapter

2   Hidden Pain

Milly Snodgrass was a sad little creature.   And long before Franny had moved to Nit Picky, home of the Fighting Tomcats, Milly's classmates had often tormented her without pity. Even though Milly had been with the same group of kids since first grade, her sense of belonging was still below sea level.

To look at Milly's physical appearance, one would wonder why she was so mistreated by the others. Unlike Franny, Milly was a beautiful child. She had long auburn hair, blue eyes and a flawless complexion. Milly wore nice clothes; not fancy, but they were always clean and neat. She wasn't dumb either or anything like that. However, Milly was an extremely quiet girl. She was usually very withdrawn from the others. Seldom did she smile or, for that matter, speak to her classmates.

The unkind teasing by the Nit Picky kids had only made Milly pull deeper into her personal shell. The kids had made no secret of their nickname for her, "Snody". Many times they sent her home in tears.

One would've thought that the boys in Milly's class would have defended a pretty girl like her. But, at that age, the Nit Picky boys, for the most part, weren't particularly fond of girls. In fact, some of the boys still believed that their lives might have been better if the good Lord had left girls off the planet all together. Of course, there were girls who felt the same way toward the boys.

Tormenting girls was the boys' job, it seemed, particularly if the girl looked or acted different than the rest. Even the girls in Milly's class were often horribly unkind to their own gender. This was especially true if the girl happened to be prettier or smarter than they were; Milly was both. All of that being the case, not one boy or girl in the Nit Picky Grade School ever had attempted to find out why Milly was so shy, or "stuck-up" as they called it. But when Franny moved to town and started school, things began to change for the better for Milly and her classmates. Franny was like a ray of golden sunlight.

This "sunlight" was due to Franny's love for Christ and His love filling her heart. She seemed wise beyond her years in her care for others. Perhaps some of the difference that Franny made at Nit Picky came from her own victories in Christ. After all, Jesus had helped her overcome the ugliness that others had shown toward her. No doubt Franny's knowledge that Jesus loved her in spite of her flaws accounted for much of her gentle and loving behavior. At one time Franny had felt that only her family loved her. She knew that she wasn't pretty compared to other children and that her athletic skills were non-existent. She realized that she was imperfect. However, from the time that Franny discovered Christ's love, she learned to see herself and others in a more positive way. Franny had made up her mind to share that love with everyone she met.

Franny had adopted the following Scripture verses as her life's goal: "Therefore, as God's chosen people, holy and dearly loved, clothe yourselves with compassion, kindness, humility, gentleness and patience. Bear with each other and forgive whatever grievances you may have against one another. Forgive as the Lord forgave you. And over all these virtues put on love, which binds them all together in perfect unity." (Colossians 3:12-14) She tried to live the truth of those verses.

For Milly Snodgrass, however, things were quite different in her life, especially at home. It was there that she felt unloved most of all. When Milly told her mother how the school children treated her, her mom laughed. She told Milly that she probably deserved their abuse because she was a troublesome child. More than once Milly's mom told her that she regretted having a child. Milly stopped saying anything to her mother about being mistreated at school. In fact, Milly did her best to say nothing at school or at home. She played, studied, hurt, and cried alone.

Once, while playing in the backyard, Milly fell; her mother told her that she couldn't be bothered right then and not to cry so much. Milly didn't get a hug, not even a tissue to dry her tear-soaked face. On another occasion while Milly was

playing in her home, she accidentally knocked over her mother's favorite lamp. Milly trembled with fear as she cleaned up the broken pieces. When mother came home from work, she quickly noticed the missing lamp and spotted the bag of pieces by the table. Immediately she flew into a raging fit. No matter how many times Milly told her that she was sorry, her mother continued to yell all the more.

Milly's mother screamed, "I will never forgive you. That lamp was given to me as a graduation present from my mother! I told you that she died suddenly only a month later!" Milly's mother raged on until she grew hoarse.

Poor Milly didn't believe that she was loved at home or at school. She felt that her young heart resembled the shattered lamp that her mom had tossed out the door. A day or so after the lamp episode, Milly met the new kid in school, Franny. It was lunch hour and, of course, Milly was sitting by herself, partly by choice and partly because the other kids chose to avoid her.

"Let Miss 'Snody' sit by herself," taunted the kids.

But Franny didn't join in. It hadn't taken her long to notice Milly's isolation. Franny, with all her inabilities, wasn't the least bit shy. She simply took her sack lunch, consisting of a peanut butter and jelly sandwich, an apple, and a carton of chocolate milk, and she plopped right down beside Milly. The other children's eyes grew large in shock as they wondered how Milly would react to the new girl. Startled by Franny's sudden appearance, the lonely girl paused for a moment and then went on with her lunch. The kids thought that Milly would stick her nose in the air and move to another table. But she didn't; she just sat there. Actually, Milly was surprised that anyone would sit down with her; it was nice for a change.

The pain of neglect that Milly felt was understandable to Franny. She had been victim to that feeling herself and made the first move to get acquainted with Milly. Friendship, however, didn't happen in a day or two, but with persistence and patience, Franny earned Milly's trust.

Milly eventually opened up to her new friend. She told Franny everything about the hurts that she had experienced at home and at school. Milly began to realize that Franny was different because of her relationship with Jesus. Franny helped Milly to understand that Christ's love and care for others included kids just like her.

With Franny's lead in befriending Milly, the other Nit Picky kids began to see that she wasn't so stuck up after all. When they saw Milly laughing at Franny's antics, they wanted to be included too. In time Milly's shield of protective silence was chipped away and she had lots of friends.

All of Milly's problems didn't suddenly disappear. Her mother didn't become loving overnight, but Milly had discovered a love in Jesus that she had never dreamed possible. She too accepted Jesus into her heart like Franny. Milly's attitude toward her mother improved. Milly also tried to help her mother feel loved. In the months ahead, Milly learned that her own dad had deserted them when she was born. He had run off one night leaving mother with a newborn baby and nothing to live on. Her mother had always told Milly that her father had died in Korea and was buried there. Milly's mother had become very bitter. She had also felt unloved and, in part, blamed Milly.

In the years that followed, Milly's mother gradually came to accept the love of Christ that she saw in her daughter, Franny and others. She sought help in dealing with her anger.

One day, late in Milly's senior year, she came in from school to find her mother holding a brightly wrapped package. "Here Milly," she said, "this is for your graduation." The card was addressed: "To My Beloved Daughter." Opening the card Milly read, "Dear Milly, I forgave you long ago for breaking the lamp. Can you ever forgive me for my flawed behavior toward you? Love, Mother".

"Yes, Mother, I can and I have," Milly said. With tears in her eyes, she opened the box to find a beautiful lamp. On its base was the figure of an angel patting the head of a lamb. Milly knew that the angel represented her mom and the lamb represented her and that, without a doubt, Christ's love had healed their broken relationship forever.

Chapter

3   **The Bully**

Nobody really liked Ned; he made sure of that. In fact, Ned seemed quite proud of his unfavorable disposition. He'd been a classmate to the Nit Picky gang since the second grade. Most of his classmates wished that he had moved anywhere except Nit Picky. They wanted to leave him behind another grade or two. By third grade, Ned had already earned the nickname of "Nasty", "Nasty" Ned Knarley. He was so despicable that rumor was the family dog even hid when he came home.

Ned had coal-black hair and narrow, beady eyes. He despised his pug nose and pointed chin. "Nasty" was built solid, but his ears were a bit oversized for his heart-shaped head. He was missing a couple of teeth, knocked out in a fight. The truth was that he looked mean on the outside because of the hatefulness on his inside.

Ned would sneak a chew of tobacco when he could snitch some; he liked to spit it in front of the girls. Their looks of disgust seemed to thrill his nasty heart. Ned found a cigarette on the ground one time and chewed it up right in front of Susy. It made her so sick that she had to leave school. "Nasty" would purposely trip kids in his class as they went to the chalkboard. He'd get caught at times and sent to the office, but he appeared to enjoy that. He claimed that he could take ten whacks of Principal Straightshooter's paddle and never even flinch. He was in the office so often that he had his own desk there.

"Nasty" liked nothing better than to torment other kids and pick fights. Usually it was with those he knew he could easily whip. In fact, Ned had been known to kick a fireplug or two just because they were in his way. He grumped and growled, jumped and snarled at everyone that drew a breath in Nit Picky, home of the Fighting Tomcats. Some of the class joked that Ned's picture should replace their Tomcat emblem.

Franny believed Ned boasted of his toughness because he was a sad and lonely boy on the inside. Most likely he was insecure and used his mean behavior to conceal his fears and weaknesses. She felt sympathy for him. She would have befriended him if he'd allowed her to. Whether or not Franny was right about Ned's life was not to be known for years. For the time being, all the kids were to see was Ned's nasty side.

His behavior was in stark contrast to Franny's. She had been pretty much accepted by her classmates, especially after Phil had made friends with her. Despite her lack of physical beauty, Franny had a loving charm that had earned her many friends in the several months she'd been at Nit Picky.

Perhaps Ned heard about Franny's sympathy for him and was angered by the truth of what she had said. Maybe he was envious of her large circle of friends because he only had one friend, himself. Whatever the reason, "Nasty" Ned turned his ugliness toward Franny.

One day, Franny and Milly were going upstairs to class when Ned came speeding by. He knocked Franny's books down the steps and yelled, "Ugly," all in one swift move. He paused at the top step glaring at Franny. He waited for her to yell or cry or scream. She did none of those things. Ned was disappointed.

The next day it was the same story, only this time Ned was in the hall where the eighth grade boys gathered. They laughed when once again Franny's books went sailing. Sometimes people laugh at the wrong things; some of them quickly apologized to Franny and helped her pick up the mess. Milly and Phil were amazed at how Franny remained silent, as she calmly gathered her belongings.

Franny was determined not to show anger towards Ned. She had been praying for him, as well as for her own attitude toward him. The Lord led Franny to two Bible verses that really helped her deal with Ned's bad behavior. The first was "Love is patient, love is kind. It does not envy, it does not boast, it is not proud. It is not rude, it is not self-seeking, it is not easily angered, it keeps no record of wrongs." (I Corinthians 13: 4–5) And the second verse was "... If someone strikes you on the right cheek, turn to him the other also." (Matthew 5:39b)

By the third day, "Nasty" Ned had become desperate to get the best of Franny. He waited until she and her friends were crossing the dusty ball diamond on their way home. Then he raced at her! Not only did he send Franny's books flying, but he knocked her into the dust as well. Once again, as difficult as it was, she remained cool. To Ned's amazement, Franny calmly got up, brushed herself off, and picked up her books. Looking straight at Ned, Franny's eyes filled with sympathy instead of the anger and tears that Ned had expected.

Franny finally spoke, "Ned, I feel so sorry for you. To think that a big, strong, and smart boy like you has to prove himself by knocking a weak person like me into the dirt is very sad. God has given you so much potential, why are you wasting it on such foolish behavior?" She continued, "I am praying for you, Ned Knarley. For I believe that beneath that tough exterior of yours is someone who needs to be loved. Jesus loves and cares about you, and so do I." Then, rejoining her friends, Franny headed home. Ned stood there alone and dumbfounded.

Now Milly and Phil couldn't stand it! They chimed in together, as if rehearsed, "Why didn't you clobber 'Nasty'?"

To their surprise, Franny looked at them straight on and said with a Christ-like tenderness in her voice, "Why should I? Ned's doing a good job of clobbering himself. Besides," she said, "I've found its hard to hate someone that I'm praying for."

14

Having used up his best efforts to make Franny angry without success, "Nasty" Ned moved on to others who would respond as he wished. He never bothered Franny again; in fact, he became more civil acting toward her.

Ned moved away the summer before ninth grade. The kids lost track of him. Years later it was learned that he had been killed in Vietnam. His widow received his Purple Heart for bravery. Word had it that Ned sacrificed his life to save several others in his platoon. Maybe Franny's stinging words and heart-felt prayers had touched Ned after all.

Chapter

4   **Tight Pants**

    To understand this story, one must remember that the Nit Picky Grade School, home of the Fighting Tomcats, consisted of the first eight grades. When one graduated from the eighth grade, they went off to high school some few blocks away.

    For one to reach eighth-grader-hood was the ultimate. It was the peak of grade school success. As a lower grader your one dream was to become a "big" eighth grader. For it was then that you became the number one Tomcat, the top banana, the big-cheese, the head-honcho, and the leader of the pack.

    Eighth graders promoted certain myths. One was that they were to be treated like kingfish by every lower grader. Another was that no one was to ever talk back to an eighth grader because their words were the "law".

    However, the glory of the eighth graders, like all things in life, only lasted but a short time. They all knew that when their freshman year rolled around it would be back to small potatoes.

    One of the eighth grade boys by the name of Hank had a

super bad case of big-man-on-campus syndrome. Hank's grades were near the top of his class and the girls adored him. He was class president and the captain of the Fighting Tomcats' baseball team. Besides all of that, Hank had the main part in the Nit Picky Grade School's spring play, *"The Rise and Fall of Glory"*. He was leading "man" to one of the cutest girls in the eighth grade, "Cutesy" Kelly Stearnfellow.

Hank began to dress real slick with a sharp looking flattop haircut, spit-polished shoes, and snug-fitting dress slacks. He began to strut around like a barnyard rooster. All of Hank's successes had gone straight to his head. He shunned his one-time friends in the lower grades, reasoning that he was too important to mingle with them. Hank even began to treat his fellow eighth graders like they were beneath him. He only acted friendly to those few who made him feel important or that could be used for his benefit. He didn't spend time with the Nit Picky gang anymore. After all, most of them did nothing to enhance his position, many of them were seventh graders, and many of them wore patched blue jeans. When he did speak to them, it was usually in arrogant tones. The shunned friends gave Hank a new name; they called him "Haughty", "Haughty" Hank.

Perhaps the one Hank snubbed the most was his friend Franny. They had become such good friends in the time that she had lived in Nit Picky. One day however, when Franny invited Hank to get an ice cream pushup at Charlie's, "Haughty" was quick to inform her that he no longer visited such lowly establishments. With arrogant tones, Hank said, "I only go to places that serve **Mega Superior Ice Cream**; you know the brand, shipped in from Chicago. It's the number one ice cream in the nation." Locally it was only served in **The Par Excellence Restaurante** located in Wicksburg.

"Besides, Franny," Hank said in his lofty voice, "I don't think we should be seen together anymore. It wouldn't be good for my image. I've moved up the society ladder you know. No offense." Then he strutted off.

Franny stood there in shock as her downcast eyes leaked tears of sadness. Her heart ached as if it had been kicked. "Haughty" Hank was also snobbish with most of the rest of the

17

Nit Picky gang. He became the ball team's "Mr. Bigshot", and was hurting the team. They had lost the last three games; team spirit was at its lowest. Hank was trying to be a one-man show.

Finally, he was summoned to the principal's office. "Hank," Mr. Straightshooter began, "to be blunt, you've developed a bad case of 'the big-head syndrome'." He said, "The faculty and student body have had it up to their eyeballs with your arrogant behavior. Why, if your head gets any larger, we'll have to special order your ball cap." Mr. Straightshooter went on and on and on, giving Hank a stern father-like talking to.

Well! Hank had had all of Mr. Straightshooter that he could take. For, after all wasn't he, Hank, an eighth grader, the president of his class, the ball team's captain and so forth. He wasn't going to be subjected to such verbal abuse; Mr. "Haughty" Hank stormed out of the principal's office in a huff!

"I'll just show them all," he grumbled. "I'm needed and important; I am, after all, the star of the spring play. They had better watch how they treat me," he continued as he resumed his distinctive strut back to the classroom.

When Hank showed up for play practice that night, he was shocked to find that his leading "lady" had changed. Kelly had fallen that afternoon at home and had broken her left arm, right leg, and blacked both eyes. She would be out of school for days. Mrs. Playwright, the drama coach, had brought in Franny, who had been learning the part as Kelly's understudy, just in case of such a crisis.

Hank was furious! "How can this be?" he questioned. "How can I, such a fine looking eighth grader, be leading man with 'Flawed' Franny, a seventh grader?" But he had no choice.

Hank muttered to himself, "Poor Franny will look so bad next to my grand performance." He doubted her ability to know her lines, and besides, she was just 'not so good looking' compared to his charming self. "No doubt I will have to carry the play myself or it will be ruined." he concluded. But, over the next few nights, play practice went better than Hank had expected. "At least Franny knows her lines," he mumbled under his haughty breath.

The night of the play arrived, and most of Nit Picky

showed up to see the kids' performance. Even Mayor Bob Dooalot, Hank's uncle, was there. The lights went down, the curtain went up, and acts one and two sailed by smoothly. The third act began with Hank's character "Demetrius" entering with his drawn sword (wooden, of course) to rescue the fair damsel, "Angelica", played by Franny. Hank twirled his sword, a move that he had added, but it slipped out of his hand and flew across stage, barely missing Franny's nose. Hank scurried to retrieve it, regroup his grand style, and spew forth his next lines. He did all of this as if his strange moves had been planned.

As Hank bent over to retrieve his fallen sword, the backside of his skin-tight pants split from top to bottom. The ripping sound was so loud that it brought a gasp from the audience. They thought that surely the curtains were tearing from their cables. Hidden waist down by a fake bush, Hank was safe for the moment. The crowd seemed to relax a bit, but not Hank. With his face as red as a freshly polished fire engine, Franny realized his predicament. Hank stared at Franny with a look that indicated he had not only lost his modesty, but he had lost his lines, his courage, and was about to 'exit stage left'. Fast-thinking Franny began to ad-lib in character as "Angelica".

"Oh 'Demetrius'," she began, "Did thou hear that horrid tearing sound? It must mean the approach of that evil one, 'Lantus,' (being played by "Clutts" Clinkmyer). "Clutts" waited offstage to see how Hank and Franny were going to get out of this mess so he could make his entrance. He was also trying to muffle his laughter at Hank's exposed Superman undies.

On stage, Hank stammered, trying to get his composure and hide his vast exposure all at the same time. He replied to Franny's ad lib, "Yes, ...um...that is...ah...Lan---tus, yes, it must be he... or him!".

"'Demetrius', my beloved," 'Angelica' continued, "ye must save me from that tyrant, 'Lantus'! For he is a treacherous king." Moving toward Hank as she spoke, Franny removed her sweater-like garment. "Here, my beloved, wrap this covering around thy waist, for it will bring thee good luck. It will remind thee of my devoted love as ye fight that evil 'Lantus.'"

Hank, catching on to what Franny was doing, happily

19

covered his gapping pants by wrapping the sweater around his waist and securing it's sleeves with a tight knot. At last the tear in his pants was hidden. Then with renewed confidence, Hank stepped from behind the fake bush in character as "Demetrius". Mrs. Playwright was laughing herself to tears as she helplessly watched Franny trying to pull the play back on track.

Having realized that the character "Angelica" had given him his cue, the wicked and evil "Lantus" ("Clutts"), entered the stage with his sword raised high. The play continued as written with "Demetrius" defeating the horrible "Lantus". "Demetrius" was made king and took "Angelica" to be his queen. They lived happily ever after in make-believe-land. The curtain closed.

The townsfolk clapped and cheered for the kids' performance, never really knowing what had happened to Hank. "Bravo! Bravo!" bellowed the standing Mayor Bob Dooalot. He always did love being seen and heard.

Hank dashed for the exit and made a speedy retreat homeward. Arriving there before his parents allowed Hank to change clothes. He kept the torn-pant episode a secret from them for years. Mrs. Playwright mended the costume and nothing more was said about it. However, something else ripped that night that would take more than needle and thread to mend. It was Hank's pride.

When Hank reached his room that night, he pulled off Franny's garment of salvation. A small booklet fell from its inner pocket. Hank realized that it was Franny's little New Testament that she forever carried with her. He opened its worn pages and found marks and notes everywhere. But it was the extra page at the back that caught his attention. At its top, in huge letters, Franny had printed the word **Pride.** Beneath it she had written the following verses: "Pride goes before destruction, a haughty spirit before a fall." (Proverbs 16:18) "For everyone who exalts himself will be humbled, and he who humbles himself will be exalted." (Luke 14:11)

Tears fell from Hank's not-so-haughty cheeks as he thought how his pride had led him to treat his friends in such a horrible way, especially Franny. He hurt all the more as he thought how, in spite of his bad behavior, Franny had lovingly rescued him from his embarrassing situation. "Why was Franny so good to me after I've been such a jerk to her?" he wondered.

Hank knew that his pride had truly preceded his fall, but now it was time to make amends. He decided not only to apologize to Franny when he returned her possessions, but also to find out more about the truths in her little Bible. Hank really wanted to know what it was that made Franny so different. She had proved what a true Christ-like friend was all about.

Hank learned his lesson about pride that spring; some folks never do. It was a few days after the play that Hank learned how Franny had even persuaded the cast to promise to keep quiet about his torn pants. That feat was perhaps Franny's most difficult accomplishment of all. She had promised them all an ice cream cone at the "What-A-Burger." It had taken all the funds she had been saving for a new dress.

After accepting Franny's Jesus into his heart, Hank became better known as "Humble" Hank. When at times he'd catch himself letting pride slip back in, he remembered the sacrifices that both Christ and Franny had made for him. And, oh yes, he never did wear tight pants again.

Chapter

5   Too Much Cooked Goose

Ruthie was a pretty little girl with dark eyes and brown hair usually in a ponytail. However, beneath that charming surface lay an ugliness that frequently escaped by way of her tongue. Her ponytail would toss to and fro when her tongue started "wagging". Her eyes would sparkle with a spiteful gleam. Ruthie would become so excited sharing a piece of "juicy" gossip that her whole body would actually prance.

Ruthie spent a great deal of time using her tongue to verbally "slice" others into little pieces. It seemed that she ran her tongue from sun up to sun down. Word had it that she even gossiped in her sleep. One of her two sisters told Phil, who told "Clutts" Clinkmyer, who then told Franny, that Ruthie's "sleep-gossiping" had become so bad they'd asked their parents if she could have a separate bed room.

When Ruthie moved to Nit Picky a year prior to this incident, it hadn't taken the kids long to find out that her cuteness was only surface deep. They had learned that her tongue was as sharp as a king's sword and as harsh as a winter storm.

One day, shortly before Easter vacation, the Nit Picky gang was eating lunch and talking about school, sports, and holiday plans, when Ruthie butted in and blurted out, **"He just cooks my goose!"**

At first the kids thought she was talking about her dad cooking the Easter goose or something, but they soon realized that she meant nothing of the kind. She was talking about one of their classmates, Lonnie Mossberry, who was absent that day due to illness.

"Ruthie, what do you mean?" Franny asked, soon regretting that she had done so.

"Well," Ruthie began, "Lonnie simply burns me up because he is always so 'nicey-nice' to our English teacher, Mrs. Playwright. Everyone knows that!" exclaimed Ruthie. "And that old nag is the meanest teacher in this school. Why she 'cooks my goose' almost as much as Lonnie does. She's always fussing at me for not having my homework on time. She continually 'shushes' me when I talk during study hall. She even had the nerve to send me to the office for being tardy the other day. Doesn't she know this is almost the Sixties?" Ruthie stormed on, "The nerve of Lonnie giving her a thank you note for helping him with his English paper. Lonnie just wants to be Teacher's Pet! You all see that, don't you? Well, don't you?"

Pausing only briefly for a quick refill of air, Ruthie ranted on in her dramatic style, "It really 'grates my potatoes' and 'ruffles my tail feathers' that Lonnie told Mrs. Playwright that he understood grammar better from her teaching than ever before. I can't stand him or her!" exclaimed the red faced Ruthie.

Just when the gang thought they could actually speak again, old "Rant'n" Ruthie revved her tongue once again.

"And another thing," her tongue wagged on, "I thought I'd explode when Lonnie opened the door for teacher Bradshaw the other day. Mr. Bradshaw is old enough to open his own door, even with a broken leg, crutches, and one arm in a sling. Lonnie even helped him carry some books into his room. He just wants extra points, that's all." By this time Ruthie had worked herself into quite a tizzy. She exclaimed, "Lonnie Mossberry 'cooks my goose' so much that it makes me want to scream!"

And scream she did, right there in the Nit Picky lunchroom, in front of God and everybody. She let out the most blood-curdling, hair-raising scream the gang had ever heard. It nearly gave the lunchroom monitor, Mr. Bradshaw a stroke, as if he needed any thing else to go wrong. It startled Susy so much that she dropped her chocolate milk, which shot up its straw and hit "Clutts" Clinkmyer in his right eye. "Clutts" then fell against Milly, who jerked and bumped her knee against the table. In doing so, she knocked over the pepper shaker. Sid took such a sneezing fit that it made his nose bleed and he had to see the nurse. "Rant'n" Ruthie had everyone's attention all right. She just smiled her "pleased-with-herself smile".

Following her "glass-breaking" scream, Ruthie said, "I feel like I ought to give Lonnie a piece of my mind; he's making the rest of us look bad, and I'm 'man' enough of a woman to tell him." But everyone knew she was bluffing. She wouldn't say anything to him, it wasn't Ruthie's style. She simply enjoyed talking about others behind their backs. Mr. Bradshaw scolded Ruthie for her outburst in the lunchroom, but it had no effect.

Later, Phil told the gang, "Ruthie's sudden scream must have been her tongue stretching exercise; not that she needs it."

They all laughed, except Sid; he still had cotton up his nose. And that was only one incident with "Rant'n" Ruthie. That's what the kids of Nit Picky, home of the Fighting Tomcats, had named her. But Ruthie didn't care what they called her; she never had a good word about any of them anyway. The kids joked that Ruthie must have a goose haven in her back yard since someone was always cooking one.

The children gave Ruthie as much space as possible. The gang all knew that she could out talk any three of them combined; generally it was all negative. The Nit Picky kids learned that when Ruthie talked to someone, the ones not present were the topic of conversation. They disliked Ruthie's constant tongue wagging and people-bashing, but there seemed to be no cure for her personality flaw.

After Easter break, Ruthie's desk sat empty. The kids were glad for the silence from her corner. However, by the second day of her absence, Franny asked Mrs. Playwright about Ruthie. Her teacher said that Ruthie had been in the hospital at Wicksburg over Easter break for an emergency operation on her

24

stomach. Franny suggested that the class make up some get well cards and take them to her. The class hissed and booed the idea. However, Mrs. Playwright thought it was a splendid idea and made it a writing assignment. She would make the first card herself, to set the example.

Two days later the kids were told that Ruthie almost died from complications. She would have to stay in the hospital a little longer. When the gang realized the serious condition of their classmate, they were glad about making the cards. The Nit Picky gang had learned enough kindness from Franny that they didn't wish anyone harm, even Ruthie.

Unsure of how she would receive the cards, Franny, "Clutts", and Phil were elected to visit Ruthie in the hospital and deliver them. Phil's mother drove the kids to Wicksburg. They had to secure a special pass to go to the second floor where Ruthie was recuperating. Surprised, but pleased to see them, she invited them in. Ruthie had realized how lonely it was to be away from her classmates. She hadn't expected their visit because of the distance, and because of the bad things she had said about them. She knew that they couldn't possibly like her.

Ruthie began to cry when she read the homemade cards from her classmates and Mrs. Playwright. Phil told Ruthie that many of the kids, and Mrs. Playwright too, had been praying for her. Franny said that the class was sad that she had to have surgery and missed being at home for Easter. Franny talked to Ruthie about Jesus' love for everyone---including her. "Clutts" explained to her how Christ had died on the cross for all of them and had risen from the dead on the third day.

"That was the first Easter morning," Franny added. Then she shared with Ruthie how Jesus had even offered forgiveness from that cross for the very ones who had placed him there.

Ruthie said that she realized all of that, and she knew that she'd not behaved like she should. She explained to her visitors that the doctor discovered that she had a serious ulcer. "He told me," she said, "that, without a doubt, it had been irritated by my negative attitude toward others. My parents had informed the doctor about my bad behavior."

Franny read Bible verses from the book of James 3:5-6:

25

"Likewise the tongue is a small part of the body, but it makes great boasts. Consider what a great forest is set on fire by a small spark. The tongue also is a fire, a world of evil among the parts of the body. It corrupts the whole person, sets the whole course of his life on fire, and is itself set on fire by hell."

Ruthie admitted that that fire had been hot enough to burn a hole in her stomach and she was truly sorry for her ugly words about others. Ashamed of her nickname, she promised that with Jesus' help she would not be a "Rant'n" Ruthie any longer.

Once she was back in school, the children treated Ruthie kindly, a lot better than she had ever treated them. She was grateful for their help and friendship. When she'd start to say "cooks my goose," the Nit Picky gang was quick to remind her of the ulcer and God's love.

With the help of Jesus, along with Franny and the gang's encouragement, Ruthie eventually learned better control over her tongue. She realized that part of her problem had been her unhappiness with who she was, which had resulted in her putting others down. When Ruthie understood how much Jesus loved her in spite of her bad behavior, she started to feel better about herself. She began to look beyond the flaws of others. In doing so she discovered the joys of being herself and of having friends.

Over the years that lay ahead, Ruthie became as pretty on the inside as she was on the outside. The only "cooked goose" she ever mentioned was the one for their Easter dinner. Eventually, Ruthie grew up, married, and had five children--- but that's another story.

Chapter

6 Nit Picky Goes to Chicago

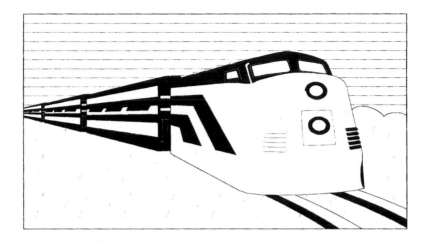

The annual Book Fair at Chicago's Museum of Science, Arts and History was fast approaching and kids at Nit Picky Grade School were counting the days in anticipation of their big trip. Most of them had never been any farther north in Illinois than Springfield. Now they were not only going to Chicago, but they were going by train.

The big night came at last. The upper-graders along with Principal Straightshooter, Mrs. Playwright the English teacher, Mr. Gravity Moore the Science teacher, and a few parents all stood huddled in the old Nit Picky Railroad Station. It had been reopened just for this special train stop. There wasn't any heat in the old building, and the kids shivered in the cold night air.

"Here it comes!" yelled the excited children. The **Chicago Jet Stream Express**, with its headlamp flashing back and forth, gleamed in the moonlight as it eased into the station. "Shuuuuer-reeeck", the train groaned to a stop.

27

"Biggest thing to happen in Nit Picky in years," exclaimed Mayor Bob Dooalot. He had come to see everyone off and to be seen. The only thing missing that night was the band, but then most of them were going on the trip.

It would take all night to reach the big and windy city. None of the students had ever been to the Chicago Museum except for "Seenit-Donethat" Susy. Usually every class had one like her. The kids knew Susy all too well. She had been a part of their class since first grade. According to Susy, she had seen and done everything and had been everywhere. Susy was positive that there was nothing she didn't know or couldn't do better than everybody else. Yep, that was Susy all right. She quickly assumed the position of the "let me tell you" information station. The Nit Picky group was in for a very LONG trip.

Because Susy had done all there was to do in Chicago as she saw it, she painted a very negative picture of how everything there was "so-o-o-o bor-i-n-g". Of course she had been able to see and do things on her trip that the group would not get to see or do on theirs. Susy was like a thunderstorm on a wiener roast. And before the kids drifted off to sleep, Susy had killed much of their enthusiasm for the next day. Most of the Nit Picky gang pretended to sleep in hopes that Susy would cease her "yapping".

Sunlight poked through the train windows as the kids stretched and made ready to unload at the Chicago station. "Seenit-Donethat" Susy jostled her way to the head of the coach so she could lead the way, of course.

When they finally reached the museum, they were amazed at its hugeness. It was packed with all sorts of stuff from a submarine to dinosaur skeletons. Oh yes, there were the book exhibits too. Susy wasn't seeing too much of any of it however, for she was too busy telling everyone what was in the next room.

Getting bored as tour guide to kids who really were doing their best to ignore her, Susy decided to explore on her own. "Who needed to see this same old stuff anyway?" she said to herself. Slipping away from the group, she found some new nooks and crannies that she hadn't covered when she was there before. Caught up in her own little tour, she drifted further and further from her classmates.

Suddenly, Susy felt a hand on her shoulder! It belonged to a tall and scary stranger; his grip was firm. He bent over and whispered that if she tried to run or scream he would make her very sorry. She felt tears welling up as she tried hard not to shake. Just as they passed the stuffed elephant display, she and her unwanted escort ran smack into Franny, Phil, Sid, Milly, and the whole Nit Picky gang.

"Where have you been, Susy?" shouted the chorus of voices, including that of Mr. Straightshooter. In the meantime, the stranger bolted for the exit. Teacher Moore was quick to see what was happening and summoned a nearby guard. Together they caught the man who, unlucky for him, had caught his coattail in the revolving exit bars.

The trip home was more exciting than ever imagined as Susy described her terrifying experience. Of course she got a good talking to by the adults, but she had already learned her lesson that day. She realized that no person is ever so smart or important that they don't need the help and friendship of others. Susy promised herself and the gang that she would never pull a stunt like that again. She apologized for being such a know-it-all. Time proved that she was sincere.

Franny said that they all needed to realize that in life, everyone needs a friend. She told the gang that Jesus and the church family were important to guide them through their lives. "God didn't create us to go without him," she said. Then Franny read from her Bible; "Just as each of us has one body with many members, and these members do not all have the same function, so in Christ we who are many form one body, and each member belongs to all the others." (Romans 12:4-5) Franny always did carry her small New Testament.

When the excited kids told Susy about all the things they had seen and done that day, she realized that she actually hadn't seen it and done that as much as she'd thought. And the long ride home? Well, it proved to be much more pleasant than any of them could have ever imagined.

Chapter

7   Cemetery Hill

Just north of the Nit Picky Grade School, home of the Fighting Tomcats, loomed "THE HILL", the cemetery hill. Compared to the Ozark Mountains, Nit Picky's hill was quite small. However, to the local kids, it was a mountain that jutted straight out of the town's flatness. The Nit Picky gang found it to be a place of great fascination because it was covered with aged gravestones, moss covered tombs, twisted cedar trees, and winding roadways paved with gravel.

"THE HILL" was the steepest part of the ridge that bordered that end of town. It was a great place for would-be "explorers" in the summer and for death defying sled sliders in the winter. Perhaps most important to the boys of Nit Picky, it was the testing grounds for one's true manliness.

Folks had to cross a small one-lane bridge that spanned the town's creek to get to the hill's base. When a kid stood on that bridge and looked straight up the gravel road, it appeared to touch the clouds. The road was narrow and covered with golf ball-sized, reddish gravel that had been dredged from the local rivers. That coarse rock provided traction for burial parties in the wintry months and a rough ride the rest of the time. A caretaker's house perched on the hillside about midway up.

Now one character in Franny's class that went by the nickname of "Clutts", "Clutts" Clinkmyer to be exact, was really named Charles. No one ever used that name except for his teachers and parents. He was the person that was always chosen last for any of the children's games.

"Clutts" was the "Charlie Brown" of Nit Picky. He was so awkward that he couldn't catch a basketball in a bushel basket when it was lobbed to him from three feet away. He couldn't even walk and pat his head at the same time.

"Clutts" tried out for basketball in the sixth grade and was cut the first day. It seemed that he only had a few minor problems; for instance, he couldn't dribble, pass, or shoot the ball. The kind coach did tell Clinkmyer, however, that at least he had the practice jersey on right side out and front-wards. The five boys that "Clutts" had accidentally tripped during the team tryouts breathed a sigh of relief as the coach scratched Clinkmyer from the list. That's the way it always seemed to go for him.

When it came to the subject of girls, some of the boys in the upper grades were still put off by their existence. Others were beginning to take a liking to the "fairer gender". So it was for "Clutts". In fact, he was kind of sweet on Miss Franny, in spite of her physical problems. The deeper beauty radiating from within her heart attracted him. After all, very few of the other children, especially the girls, ever gave "Clutts" the time of day. But Franny did. Her kindness and charm were unlike any that he'd ever experienced.

The "love bug" had stung "Clutts" hard when it came to Miss Franny. However, with all the school's popular sports heroes around, what chance did he have of being Franny's special fellow? He saw himself as a real klutz and a true zero. Even his bicycle was a big brother hand-me-down.

It was late summer, only a few days after school had started, when "Clutts" got his brilliant idea. There was only one way to prove once and for all that he was a "real man". It was time that he, Charles P. Clinkmyer, took "THE HILL"! He'd prove his worth to Miss Franny and perhaps win her heart. The other kids in the class might finally respect him, too. "Clutts" thought to himself about the many boys that had become "real men" by riding their bikes down "THE HILL" and across the bridge without crashing.

After school that very day, Clinkmyer rode his blue and white-striped Schwinn bicycle toward the cemetery hill. The bike was a 26-incher which was just a tad too tall for "Clutts". The old Schwinn had balloon-type tires, a passenger rack, a chrome-wire basket in the front, and plenty of rust everywhere else. As "Clutts" slowly panted his way to the top, the cemetery caretaker drove passed him tipping his Cardinal ball cap with a smile.

"That's good," mused Clinkmyer, "now I'll have a witness if anyone doubts my eighth-grade manliness." Finally reaching the top, he caught his breath and said, "Wow! It sure is pretty up here, I can see for miles." Pointing his bike toward Nit Picky, he said to himself, "Well, 'Clutts' old boy, it's now or never. Your destiny awaits. True manhood lies before you. And dear Franny's heart hangs in the balance."

A good shove with his right foot and Clinkmyer was off. "Watch the loose gravel, push it hard, and don't be a sissy!" were thoughts that filled his mind. He shouted to the wind, "Look at me! I must be doing at least a hundred miles an hour!"

Suddenly the inevitable happened; his front tire caught in the ridge of gravel that was mounded in the middle of the road. The bike was out of control, and so was "Clutts". C-R-A-S-H! End over end, sideways, a donut spin or two, went the poor boy and his bike. To "Clutts" the crash seemed to last for an hour or more. Finally, out-sliding his bike by at least three yards, "Clutts" slid to a grinding halt! Except for his heavy breathing, there was an eerie silence in the cemetery. He lay there as if frozen, afraid to move.

Fighting back a wave of tears building behind his closed eyes, "Clutts" slowly stirred as he sensed that nothing was broken except his last speck of pride. His skin, however, hadn't faired so well. In fact, much of it had disappeared from his right arm. In its place, rock and dirt stuck to his wounded flesh.

"O-U-C-H!" "Clutts" shouted. It's a wonder he didn't wake the dead with his agonizing yells. In his angry "dance" of pain around his bike, he gave it a swift kick, and added even more pain to his tortured body.

The caretaker slowly drove his 1948 Ford pickup truck back down the hill. He knew that he shouldn't smile, but he'd seen this sight so many times before. Besides, the kid appeared to be unbroken. The man asked, "Hey, kid, are you okay?"

"Just fine, sir, just fine," replied "Clutts" with trembling lips. Blood began to trickle down his arm and stain the rocks.

"Better get home and wash that off," said the caretaker.

"Clutts" peddled the wobbly bike toward home as fast as he could. Upon his arrival, he departed the bike even before it had stopped. As the bike hit the side of the house, "Clutts" ran inside yelling, "I've got gangrene! I've got gangrene! I just know it! I saw it happen to a cowboy in the movie, *Gunsmoke at High Noon.*" Breathless, he went on, "I'm sure I'll lose my arm like he did! I don't even have a bullet to bite or his cowboy whiskey to wash my wound. I'll probably die!"

Of course "Clutts" didn't have gangrene, he didn't die, nor did he lose his arm. However, he did forfeit all hope of ever ridding himself of the name "Clutts". That dream had vanished with his skin.

How did Miss Franny take to all this news? How did she respond to "Clutts", the boy who couldn't even take "THE HILL"? Well, she had one of her heart-to-heart talks with him. She told him that he didn't need to prove himself to anyone, especially her. Most of all, Franny used the experience to teach "Clutts" that Jesus loved him in spite of his failings.

She read to him from God's word in Ephesians 2:4-5; "But because of his great love for us, God, who is rich in mercy, made us alive with Christ even when we were dead in transgressions (sins)--it is by grace you have been saved."

Franny told "Clutts", "The love of Jesus is never based on what you can or cannot do; it is based on His grace. Jesus loves you in spite of your flaws; accept that love," Franny concluded.

She made "Clutts" promise never to try a trick like "THE

33

HILL" again. Franny assured "Clutts" that her friendship, like that of Christ's, was not based on his athletic skills or his ability to take "THE HILL". It was centered on who he, Charles P. Clinkmyer, was on the inside. Then Franny leaned over and kissed "Clutts" right square on the cheek as she reminded him, "Jesus loves you, and so do I."

"Clutts" gained something from that crash after all. He learned to love himself and to love others for who they are and not what they can do.

By the way, "Clutts" didn't wash his cheek for a whole week. He wouldn't have then if his mother hadn't made him.

Chapter

8   **The Big Race**

Nit Picky's location was far enough south that winter usually waited a bit longer to make its arrival. That fact allowed the annual soap-box-derby to be held the first Saturday of each November. The derby was the biggest event of the town's fall festival. It was one of the kids' grandest times in all of Nit Picky, home of the Fighting Tomcats. Kids would work for weeks building their homemade soapbox racers. The race was held on a portion of Highway 78 located at the northern edge of town. It was known as "Spill-Bottom" Hill. Legend was that its

name came from a deadly crash of a huge grain truck.
Supposedly the truck lost its brakes on the steep hill and flipped over on the sharp curve at its base, burying the driver in corn. The highway cut through the western end of the town's cemetery, thus providing some eeriness for the racers as they sped past the giant gravestones and statues.

For this one-day event, traffic had to be diverted several miles around the race area. This annual inconvenience always resulted in a complaint letter to the editor of *The Nit Picky Weekly Tribunal* from the town whiner, Walt Griper. The town's people laughed at the fact that they always knew when the race time was near just by Walt's yearly letter.

One of the kids who had lived his whole life in Nit Picky was Pete Ridder. The gang called him "Poor-boy" Pete. The name bothered him because of his love for his hard-working parents. He knew they tried, but couldn't make enough for the extras when it came to him and his five siblings. "Poor-boy" usually wore hand-me-down clothes, and often his jeans had patched knees, but they were always clean. However, in spite of his situation, "Poor-boy" wore a giant smile. There was one thing that he had that money couldn't buy; it was his loving family. He and his siblings had many good times that some of the richer kids never seemed to enjoy.

Pete was particularly excited about that year's race because of actions taken that fall by the Nit Picky City Council. They had decided to offer money for the race winners instead of the traditional turkeys. First place was to receive $50, second $25, and third $15. In the 1950/60's that was a heap of cash, especially for a kid like Pete. Oh yes, Walt Griper wrote another letter complaining about his tax dollars or something or other. Even though Walt was thought to be one of the richest men in Nit Picky, he was no doubt the most selfish and miserable too.

Pete reasoned that if he won the grand prize, he could give it to his mother, father, and siblings for their Christmas. Most likely it would be the only Christmas they'd have that year due to his dad's recent layoff.

Most of the Nit Picky kids weren't rich, by any means, so their soapbox cars were usually pretty well matched. But "Poor-boy's" dad didn't have much in the way of tools or know-how when it came to race cars. Pete didn't let that stop his quest to win the big race. Once signed up for the competition, he set to building his soapbox racer. He worked late into the evenings designing and building his car with his meager tools and supplies. But poor old Pete had a very serious problem. He didn't have any wheels for his car, and he didn't have any money to purchase them. Pete stewed over what to do; he just had to win

36

the race, for his family's sake.

One night Pete awoke from a dream about the race with an idea for wheels. To understand his plan one must know that in those days coffee was often purchased in large cans that had a metal key-like device attached. The key was removed and inserted near the top of the can and twisted until the whole top came off. The lid was left with a quarter inch lip on its edge. Pete reasoned that his 68 lbs. would need about ten of those lids secured together to make each wheel. He set out collecting lids from all the neighbors, who were more than glad to help him. They would simply smile a dubious smile when he eagerly explained his plans for the lids.

With only a few short days to go until the big race, Pete finally had enough lids. He fastened each set of ten lids together with four screws and mounted them to his two wooden axles. It was time for a test run down the paved road in the Catholic cemetery just west of town. Franny and the gang had taken an interest in Pete's car and his dreams for the winnings, even though some of the others were also entering the race. The Nit Picky gang gathered with Pete for his test run just one week before the race. They walked with him as he pulled his car up the steep hill. With anticipation, the kids watched him as he climbed inside the soap box car and tested the hand brake and steering. Then with baited breath, they watched as "Clutts" and Phil shoved him off.

"Yea!" the children cheered; the car was actually rolling! But their glee and Pete's smile were short-lived, for, about ten feet down the hill, his metal can-lid wheels simply folded in half. **S-c-r-u-n-c-h,** Pete felt the rough pavement grinding under his bottom as the car slid for a ways until he finally screeched to a stop! "Poor-boy" Pete cried as he slumped over the hand made steering wheel. Franny's face clouded up too, for she knew what this race meant to Pete. The kids helped Pete carry his car back to his dad's shed. He thought that it was hopeless, as he kicked one of the flattened can-lid wheels.

That day Franny called an emergency meeting of the Nit Picky gang. She was the only girl that could do that. Franny had a plan to help Pete. She told everyone of the problem: Pete

37

needed some real tires for his derby car.

Franny explained, "You all know that old Jack Bean at Jumping Jack's Pawnshop is good to buy stuff from folks in trouble; well, Pete's in trouble. I think we ought to help him by selling whatever we can to Mr. Jack."

To set the example, Franny donated her new bracelet that had been a gift on her last birthday. The other kids knew how special that was to her, so they too began to give items of great value to them. They put all their goods in a box and hauled it in Phil's old red wagon to Jumping Jack's Pawnshop.

Jack Bean smiled as the motley troop entered his door. "What can I do for you youngins today?" he boomed in his window-rattling bass voice.

Franny explained to Mr. Jack what they wanted to do as he sorted through their treasures. He had to turn away from them to wipe his moistened burly cheeks. He was touched by what the kids were doing. Their goods really weren't worth much, and Jack knew it, but he gave them to the penny of what he knew four wheels would cost them at McAbees Hardware. The kids thanked him and took the fresh crisp five dollar bill as fast as they could two doors down the street to purchase the tires.

"Clutts" volunteered to sneak the bag of wheels onto Pete's porch so he wouldn't know where they had come from. Poor choice, however, for Clinkmyer stumbled on the steps, twice going up and once coming down. The only note the kids left with the wheels said, "Win the race, Pete, these are for you." "Clutts" barely made it behind some bushes before Pete came out to see what the noise was. When he opened the mysterious bag, Pete had to rub his eyes and blink several times before he'd believe what he was seeing. Without delay, it was out to the shed, off with the crunched coffee-can-lids and on with the shiny new wheels.

The day of the big race arrived. Nit Picky shut down as folks lined the road for the race. Even old Walt Griper was spotted watching from behind a tree. There were popcorn stands, soda-pop venders, hot-dog booths, and all the makings for the festive fall event. Mayor Bob Dooalot sat as judge at the finish line. The race was soon started, and right away "Big" Butch took the lead, but Pete didn't give up, for even the second place prize would help his folks. Pete hunkered down to cut the wind resistance and kept his car steady. The crowd was going wild with cheers as the little wooden cars and drivers zigged and zagged their way down the steep hill.

Pete could hear Franny and Milly shouting above all the rest, "You can do it Pete, you can do it!"

Butch was a car length, almost two, ahead of Pete. Butch was sure that he'd win the race like he had for the past two years. His family did have money and his car was one that always had the best of everything. But overconfidence is a dangerous thing. That would prove true for "Big" Butch that day. He was so sure of himself that he didn't pay attention to his driving. As he watched the girls who were cheering him on, he failed to notice that he was running too close to the side of the road. His right front wheel caught the road's edge and had him into the straw bails before he could yell, "Daddy".

"Poor-boy" Pete zipped past him, still focused on one thing, the finish line just yards away. When he broke through the ribbon, Pete's loud "yahoo" nearly cracked the mayor's glasses. Some folks said they were sure they'd even heard old Walt clapping, although he'd never admit to it. When Mayor Bob Dooalot asked Pete what he was going to do with all that prize money, he simply smiled in a way that could have lighted all Nit Picky on a moonless night.

Come Monday morning, Mrs. Playwright told her seventh and eighth grade homeroom that she had found a large box on her steps over the weekend. Attached was a note that read, "Please see that the Nit Picky gang receives this, thank you." Phil and Franny went up and took the box back to a study table. The kids gathered around them as Mrs. Playwright, with curiosity, looked over their shoulders. When the lid was removed, there were all the items the kids had sold to "Jumping Jack's" to get Pete's wheels. Even the guys were speechless as they reclaimed their items. The note in the box was simply a scripture that said, "Cast your bread upon the waters, for after many days you will find it again." (Ecclesiastes 11:1)

The kids didn't know for years how it was that their

treasures came back to them. But Pete's folks knew; parents always know. Pete's mother had heard and seen "Clutts" place the bag on their porch. She also had noticed Pete peeking out from the living room window. She and Mr. Ridder overheard Pete tell his older brother how the Nit Picky gang had raised the money to purchase the wheels and what he planned to do about it. Pete told him to keep it a secret. Pete's plan was to give all the prize money to his folks for Christmas except for the five dollars given to Mr. Jack to redeem his friends' goods.

Pete's family had a great Christmas that year. Perhaps one of the best ever. But it was Mr. and Mrs. Ridder that received, in their estimation, the greatest gift of all. It wasn't the money, however, it was the gift of knowing what Pete's friends had done for him and what he in turn had done for them and his family. The Ridders knew that the Nit Picky gang, including their son, had experienced the great truth of Romans 12:10, which says, "Be devoted to one another in brotherly love. Honor one another above yourselves."

Pete eventually outgrew his wooden soapbox racer number 8, but he never forgot its lessons of love and sacrifice.

Chapter

9   **A New Start**

In Nit Picky, home of the Fighting Tomcats, the leaves of autumn had changed from their brilliant reds and yellows to a brownish covering over the frostbitten ground. The smell of burning leaves permeated the air. The chilled north winds iced one's breath, making it as a puff of smoke. Occasional snowflakes competed with the fallen leaves to blanket the earth as winter hinted its nearing arrival.

Halloween had been tucked into the closet; its candies devoured. Christmas was still a "kid's-year" away. And while the teachers reviewed the story of pilgrims, Indians and their historic meal, the Nit Picky gang thought of holidays and

Thanksgiving turkeys. The seventh and eighth grade classes had been challenged to bring in canned goods for the needy. Each student in the winning class would receive a free movie pass.

"Well! I don't see why we should have to bring food for people we don't even know, and besides if they'd work harder they wouldn't be so needy," exclaimed Gale Griper, Walt's daughter. Like her father, she found it to be second nature to grumble about everything. Each day when the teacher asked the children to turn in their canned goods, Gale would start a new round of complaining. Franny tried to help her see the fun it is to help others, but she wouldn't listen. Mrs. Playwright, their English and homeroom teacher, asked Gale if she could bring in at least one can of food.

Gale replied, "My daddy told me that I didn't have to, and besides, he wants to know what this has to do with school work? I'm supposed to be learning reading, writing, and math." At lunch, at break times, and even after school someone was constantly hearing Gale's bellyaching about the "cans for the needy" project. However, most of the eighth graders were excited that their class was leading the seventh grade in the food collection, even without Gale's help.

"When you're rich and have everything, I guess others don't count," said Phil, having just received his latest dose of Miss "Constant" Griper. That's the name he'd given her. The kids agreed that it was quite fitting.

Some few days before Thanksgiving break, the Nit Picky gang began to notice that Gale had stopped talking to everyone about anything. In fact, her silence was deafening. They figured that it was due to their apathy to her protests about the food drive. Her eyes had lost their fire and she seemed very distracted in class and at lunch. The kids were more thankful for her quietness than they were concerned about its cause. Two days before the children were to celebrate the Thanksgiving holiday, everyone but Gale was at school for the eighth-grade victory party. The kids wondered what had happened to her, but they didn't miss her whining. After all, she hadn't participated in the contest except to gripe and complain. The class had a very important decision to make that day. They knew that if

42

"Constant" Griper was there she would be negative to any choice they made about the food's distribution.

As the children ate cupcakes and ice cream they tossed out some names and suggestions about what to do with the groceries. They knew their teacher would have a list of names to aid in their decision. Mrs. Playwright was called from the room for a few moments. When she returned, the kids noticed that she looked rather alarmed.

"What's wrong Mrs. Playwright?" Phil asked.

"I'm afraid I have some bad news children," she said. "Our principal, Mr. Straightshooter, gave me some information that he received this morning. We think you need to know about it," she continued. "Walt Griper was seriously injured on his job some days ago and won't be able to work for weeks."

"That explains why Gale has been acting so differently lately," Franny said. "Why didn't she tell us?"

Walt worked several miles from Nit Picky and the news of his accident hadn't made the local paper. Since he wasn't the best liked fellow in the community, and his wife stayed at home, few folks knew of their plight. It turned out Walt wasn't as rich as everyone had thought. Being off work was placing him and his family in quite a needy position, especially at the holidays.

Franny and the gang were surprised at this news about Gale and her father. They were pretty shaken by the prospects of what all this meant for the eighth grader and her family. The kindness Franny had shown to others had influenced her class so much that the word of this family in trouble moved the kids to action. In spite of the way Gale and her father had behaved, they were in need.

Even though they were only children, the Nit Picky kids really did the Lord proud sometimes with their willingness to help others in spite of their faults. Franny had taught many in her class to practice the Bible verses that say: "Be kind and compassionate to one another...," (Ephesians 4:32a) and, "If your enemy is hungry, feed him; if he is thirsty, give him something to drink. In doing this, you will heap burning coals on his head." (Romans 12:20) This was a good chance to use these teachings.

Gale and her mom cried with joy when they opened the

43

door to find walking grocery bags coming into their living room. Kid after kid hidden behind the huge bags of goodies came into their house. Even "Rant'n" Ruthie and "Haughty" Hank were part of the merry food parade. "Clutts" Clinkmyer managed to spill his bag of groceries causing even Walt Griper to laugh. Some of the kids' parents and teachers carried in things like a ham and a turkey, stuffing and all the trimmings for a great Thanksgiving meal.

Mr. Walt Griper lay in his in-home hospital bed trying to hold back his emotions of both thanks and shame over his past behavior. What could his family say? "Thank you," seemed so inadequate. There was enough food to last them for several weeks. And when the parents of the eighth grade class learned what their children were doing with the food collection, they took up a money donation to help the Griper family with their bills. Mayor Bob Dooalot laughed and said that he couldn't believe he was giving money for someone like Walt Griper who had been so critical of him in the town's newspaper.

Walt, being encouraged by such kindness, continued his healing process. By that January 3rd, he was back working again on a limited basis. The Nit Picky gang knew that things don't always work out for the best when you try to help those who are unfriendly, but they were glad that it had in this case. They were happy that their help had made a real difference.

Following the Thanksgiving break, the Nit Picky kids noticed a big difference in Gale. She actually stopped her constant griping. The kind thank you letter to the paper's editor by Mr. Griper sent shock waves through the entire town of Nit Picky. Franny was thankful that the Lord had led them to be kind to the Gripers even when, at the time, it would've been much easier to have helped someone nicer.

Thanksgiving came and went that late autumn in Nit Picky. Perhaps, however, it was one that marked a new beginning in the town's growth toward kindness. They not only had said thanks that year, but they had lived it.

Chapter

10   The Christmas Flute

All the cardboard turkeys, pilgrims, and pumpkins had been taken down; Thanksgiving Day had come and gone for another year. The Nit Picky schools were back in session with only a few weeks before the Christmas programs, parties, caroling, and holidays. Even though the work-filled weeks between Thanksgiving and Christmas seemed extremely short for the teachers and parents, to the kids of Nit Picky, home of the Fighting Tomcats, they were an eternity.

Teaching, homework, and Christmas practices for the annual programs at both church and school filled the days between the end of November and December 25th. The Nit Picky kids glowed with excitement and anticipation. They knew there would be trees, treats, and toys to be enjoyed in the coming weeks. Carols and classic Christmas songs filled Nit Picky Grade School. Even its drab halls were showing the festiveness of the season. They were increasingly adorned and decked to brighten the wonder of the Christmas season.

At school and the many town churches, the kids were marched to auditoriums for those hectic and hair-pulling rehearsals of their pieces and songs. Every year it was the same: the teachers would say it was their last program, but the kids knew that they didn't mean it. There was always some mystical voice that prodded, "It will be all right, just wait and see." Without fail, the voice was correct year after year. Granted, the programs didn't always go as planned; they went nevertheless.

Sometimes the blunders and mistakes made the programs quite unique; they were also known to add a few gray hairs to the adults in charge.

The seventh and eighth graders were given the greater responsibilities in both the school and church children's presentations. That particular Christmas was no different. Rightfully so too, for the upper graders did have some talented students. Without a doubt, the one who stood out the most that year was Tess. She played the flute. In fact, she played so well that even the children of Nit Picky recognized her gift of music and had nicknamed her "Talented" Tess.

Tess's natural gift for music, combined with her hard work and love for the flute, made her quite good. She had received A+ ratings at state music contests along with several achievement awards. There was no doubt in the minds of those who heard her that Tess had a bright future in music if she desired it. To hear and watch her play was a thrill to any music lover. One could feel the care and passion she put forth with each note. For Tess, practicing the flute wasn't a chore; she actually enjoyed it. She told Franny and the gang that to play her flute was a release of her inner being. Coming from an eighth grader, that was pretty grown up stuff. Some of the kids looked at each other as if to say, what is she talking about? Because of Tess's strong and faithful interest in the flute, her parents had sacrificed to purchase one of the best instruments for her. It was her prized possession. She took excellent care of it.

Oh, some of the kids thought she was a bit touched when it came to that "holey tin tube" as they called it. They teased her for not playing with dolls and jumping ropes more. But even her critics would have agreed that she was amazing on that flute. Tess was modest about her special ability and her prized flute. She never made a big deal about any of the awards that she had received or how expensive her flute was. Another thing about Tess was that she didn't make fun of others who were less talented. Actually, most of the eighth graders seemed proud to be her classmate; she hadn't let her gift go to her head.

Tess was the youngest of three children. She had a brother Bob who was five years older. Her sister Rachel was only eighteen months her senior and kind of "boy crazy". Tess's parents didn't make a lot of money, but they loved all their children and tried to treat them equally. Since they had purchased the flute for Tess, they felt that they should also do something special for Bob and Rachel. It took a little time and some pinching of funds, but their folks purchased an important car part for Bob's old junker. And for Rachel they bought a modern stereo record player. The speakers could be set apart for better sound. Rachel loved it and how her "Elvis" sounded in stereo.

Tess's brother, for the most part, paid her no mind. He was into cars, working, eating, and dating. But her sister Rachel was up to something far different. Her eyes were into a darker shade of green than that of their physical color. She was sick of "Tess this," and "Tess that." She despised her sister's obvious talent and sweet personality. It wasn't that Rachel lacked talents of her own; she had them, but she couldn't see them because her focus was always on Tess's victories. Rachel never seemed to have a good word for her younger sibling. Tess tried to win her love and acceptance, but with no success. Little did she know how deep Rachel's jealousy would go.

With only days before the upcoming Nit Picky Christmas extravaganza, the children and teachers were working overtime to prepare for that annual event. Tess had practiced hours on the song "O Holy Night" that was to be played as the final number at the evening's program. She had it memorized and perfect to the note. Those who heard her practice said that its beauty sent cold chills tingling down their spines. But her sister closed her ears to the song and only saw red through her green eyes. That was the only trace of the Christmas spirit in Rachel's cold heart. She knew better, but jealousy had her surrounded. She had a plan that would at last bring her younger sister hurt and embarrassment. Rachel would steal Tess's flute at the last possible moment and then watch her sister fail.

The calculations for this plan had to be precise. The school program was to be on the following Monday night, one week before Christmas. Rachel knew that Saturday Tess had a dental appointment that would keep her from her beloved flute. And since their family would be attending Sunday morning services, visiting grandmother in Wicksburg in the afternoon, and returning that evening for the church's tree-decorating celebration, Rachel reasoned that Tess wouldn't have time to practice all weekend. It would be Monday before Tess would open her flute case again for one last rehearsal. Rachel knew that she had it figured correctly when she heard Tess tell her mom that the flute would be safe in her school locker.

Because Rachel had picked up Tess's books when she was ill, Rachel knew the location and combination to the locker. Stopping by the grade school and taking the flute was easy. Rachel had also figured that she might as well gain something from all her efforts. To do so, she took the stolen flute wrapped in one of her mother's finest towels, to Jumping Jack's Pawnshop on Main Street before he closed that Friday evening. Jack gave her ten dollars, way below the flute's value, but then ten dollars was a lot of money back in those days. Besides, the ten dollars would give Rachel a chance to really shine before her mom and dad. During the upcoming Sunday night's tree trimming service there was to be a special offering for a needy missionary family in Spain. Rachel would give the ten dollars to the fund and boast that she had saved it from her year's allowances. That would impress her folks, she thought. Rachel knew that Tess had only saved three dollars for the fund.

The plan was working perfectly; Rachel could hardly wait until Monday. She knew that Tess's discovery of the missing flute would come too late to do anything about it before the evening performance. Nit Picky Grade School was not noted for having a lot of extra flutes lying around, especially of that quality. Her sister would be devastated.

Saturday came and went, Sunday morning and their visit to grandmother's home also went as planned. Sunday night arrived and time for Rachel's grand offering presentation was at hand. The church sanctuary was beautiful as usual. It was trimmed in greens and reds, and the candles' glow reflected in the stained glass windows. The tree was positioned for all to see. It had lights already, but the church family would place the ornaments on it at the conclusion of the service. But first, Rev. Watchman had a special surprise for the congregation. He had asked one of their newest members, Franny Goodman, to read scripture and offer a brief devotion before the mission offering.

Franny was a bit nervous as she made her way to the podium. She was so short that Reverend Watchman had placed a wooden box behind the pulpit for her to stand on. The audience couldn't see the word "Ivory" that was printed on its sides. Franny grinned as she peered at the folks through her huge glasses. "Merry Christmas," she began. "Tonight I felt impressed not to read the traditional Christmas story." There was a gasp in the audience. Franny continued, "But for some reason, that I don't understand, the Lord wanted me to read from 1 Corinthians and Matthew. Maybe you'll know why."

She opened her Bible and read: "You are still worldly. For since there is jealousy and quarreling among you, are you not worldly? Are you not acting like mere men?" (1 Cor. 3:3) Continuing in Matthew's gospel she read: "Therefore, if you are offering your gift at the altar and there remember that your brother has something against you, leave your gift there in front of the altar. First go and be reconciled to your brother; then come and offer your gift." (Matt. 5:23-24)

Franny spoke but a moment or two about the verses, offered a sweet, child-like prayer and took her seat. In the mean time, Rachel sat petrified and pale as a ghost. She didn't even hear her mother ask if she was feeling all right. The ten-dollar bill she clutched tightly in her hand was getting soggy from her sweating palms. The Lord knew what she had done and for the first time she too realized her evil deed. But what could she do? The time of the offering was at hand. The ushers were passing the collection buckets. Her parents were watching. They had bragged on her so. Beads of sweat popped from her brow. The bucket passed and the moist ten-dollar bill was released to join its like kind. The deed was completed, but there was not one drop of happiness in her troubled heart.

The tree was trimmed, the carols were sung, the offering total announced, and they all applauded, except for Rachel. The final prayer was offered and the folks all filed out filled with Christmas joy, except for Rachel. Those scriptures filled her. Panic and fear filled her. Dread of Monday filled her. Most of

49

the night Rachel lay awake as she tried to figure how to make things right. She knew the Lord wasn't pleased with her offering; she wasn't either. She knew quite well why the Lord had led Franny to read those verses. Toward morning she finally dozed off for a short while and began to dream. She saw in her dream the baby Jesus in the manger smile as the "Little Drummer Boy" played his drum, the only gift he had to offer. But the baby cried as He looked at Rachel standing there with her ten dollars. Rachel sat upright, wide-awake; she knew what she had to do.

Monday afternoon there was pandemonium when Tess found that her flute was missing from its case. The program director almost passed out. There were tears and fears and bedlam. But at the high school, where Rachel sat, there was a calm determination for what she must do. As soon as that final bell rang, she charged out the door like a bull from a rodeo stall. As fast as she could make it home, Rachel gathered up her prized stereo and Elvis records and headed back to the pawnshop. Jack was surprised to see her again so soon. Not wasting a moment, she asked him to trade her the flute for the stereo and records. Jack smiled his profit-minded smile as he jotted down some figures. She begged him to hold on to her goods and agreed to pay him fifty cents a week until the ten dollars plus interest was paid in full. Jack warned her that if she missed one payment he would feel free to sell her goods out right.

Again, not letting the soles of her shoes cool off, she ran back to the grade school to find her sister. When she arrived, the dismay she found was staggering. Her sister's eyes were red from tears, and the kids were still fanning the director.

Rachel called Tess away from the group where they could talk. She explained the whole story and, with sincere tears of repentance, begged Tess to forgive her. Rachel then opened the cloth in her hands to reveal the prized flute. Tess cried some more, Rachel hadn't stopped sobbing. They hugged. When the kids and director heard that the flute had been found, they danced and cheered with joy. The entire scene was quite remarkable. But Tess never told them where the flute had been.

That evening Tess's family sat proud as the beautiful notes from her flute spoke of the Holy Christmas Night when the Christ child was born. The Christmas program ended, as do all events in one's life. But the lessons learned and relationships restored made that year's program the most memorable ever.

Chapter

11   Rich Boy

The winter holidays had long passed at the Nit Picky Grade School, home of the Fighting Tomcats. Hope of an early spring excited almost everyone except for a young fellow named Sid. He was a transfer student that had moved to Nit Picky a few months after Franny. Nothing ever seemed to impress, please, or excite Sid, at least it appeared that way to the Nit Picky gang. He was a "cold bird", seldom smiling. And when he did, it was more of a smirk than a smile. One felt a sense of inferiority when around Sid for very long.

The Nit Picky kids didn't accept Sid too well. The reason was obvious to everyone, except him. Simply put, he was a snob and by the way he acted, the kids didn't believe that he cared anyway. They learned that Sid was from a well-to-do family. His father was vice-president of a huge corporation that had opened a test plant in Nit Picky. Sid's family had moved there until his father could be sure the expansion was on solid footing. Unlike many of the mothers of that day, Sid's mother worked outside of the home. She had a college education and had secured a job with a legal firm in nearby Wicksburg.

From Sid's remarks, he left no doubt that he felt it was a real trial to live in a place like Nit Picky. He was accustomed to "Big City" life. Sid was always dressed in the best clothes; he sported a handsome watch and ring. Few of his classmates had such finery. In fact, Sid lacked for nothing except a likable personality. It was rumored that his family had two televisions, two automobiles, four radios, and two telephones. Sid had bragged about his stereo: he could stack six records at a time.

The gang snickered when Lonnie said, "If Sid's nose sticks any higher in the air, the door ways at Nit Picky Grade School will all have to be raised."

Sid's rejection began shortly after he arrived at Nit Picky. Unlike their other new student, Franny, Sid was rude and unfriendly. Franny had been such a good influence on the class. Because of her, the kids had actually tried to include Sid, but with no success. They soon gave up on him.

Sid left no doubt that he felt he was several degrees above the "kiddies" of Nit Picky, as he referred to them. He didn't mix with anybody. He bragged a lot to the teachers as he played up to them. They, in turn, seemed highly impressed with this finely dressed, smart, and handsome new kid.

The Nit Picky gang really felt snubbed when Sid refused at Christmas and again at Valentine's day to chip in a dollar for the teacher's present. They knew he could afford it and for most of them it was a stretch to give that much, but they did it anyway.

When the kids sent cards to some soldiers overseas at Christmas, again Sid refused to be of any help. In fact, he never participated in anything that the class tried to do for others. The kids were amazed at the difference between Sid and Franny. Sid became known as "Selfish" Sid. The kids believed he was so selfish that he probably wouldn't give his grandmother a glass of water if she had been lost in the desert for a week.

He would never give away extra milk at lunchtime. He wouldn't give anyone a stick of gum, or a jawbreaker candy, even if he had a bag full and three in his mouth. He'd never share his marbles, or anything else.

Then one day as Franny happened to be passing the semi-darkened film projection room on her way to recess, she heard someone crying. Stopping, she backed up to listen more closely. It was coming from within the film room. Hesitantly, Franny peeked into the room. She spotted Sid in a corner with his head crumpled on the chair arm, sobbing.

Franny wasn't eager to approach Sid; in the past, he had rejected her efforts to be friendly. However, it wasn't in Franny's nature to avoid a classmate in distress. She was one of those people who loved to help those in need. Franny was a great listener with an understanding heart, because she truly loved Jesus and cared about others, even "Selfish" Sid.

Sid looked up as Franny approached; quickly he wiped his tears away. She figured he'd tell her to get out. However, his sad eyes beckoned her to stay. Those dark-brown eyes appeared as open doors into his lonely heart. Sid's pent-up emotions began to gush from his quivering lips like floodwaters through a broken levee. Patiently, Franny listened, learning many things that had encouraged Sid's selfish behavior.

He was born out of wedlock to a sixteen-year-old girl. She didn't want anything to do with her child; her parents didn't either. The whole baby business had been a tremendous embarrassment to the family. Sid's father, only a child himself, fled the scene. Given away, Sid lived in one orphanage after another until age seven; he never had anyone or anything that he could call his own. Other children often avoided him like a doctor's needle because he was considered a "reject".

Even though most folks wanted to adopt a baby and didn't accept children over two years old, an older couple chose

Sid on his seventh birthday. After his adoption by the well-to-do pair, he suddenly lacked for nothing. Admitting that it was wrong, Sid told Franny that he took revenge on everyone else. He vowed that he would never give any of his money or possessions to others. He learned that it was easier to simply avoid others rather than face them and have to share or perhaps experience rejection again. However, in doing so, Sid had become terribly lonely. Recently the loneliness had become so unbearable that he was thinking about ending his life. Franny was really scared when he said that. She was afraid for him, partly because she had never heard anyone say something like that. But then, she had never met anyone who had been through what Sid had just described to her. Franny wished sometimes that she wasn't such a good listener. His story made her very sad, but she determined to do what she could.

Well, this story had a good ending, because Jesus helped Franny to convince Sid to go to her pastor for help. The pastor in turn was able to get both Sid and his adoptive parents some much-needed family counseling through a Children's Home. Franny played a key role in Sid's healing at school, too. She taught him God's Word that says "Give, and it will be given to you. A good measure, pressed down, shaken together and running over, will be poured into your lap. For with the measure you use, it will be measured to you." (Luke 6:38)

"Simply put," Franny said, "what you give is what you get in return. If you want a friend, you must be one."

Sid learned that a smile usually brought a smile and kindness generally returned kindness. It was going to take some time for Sid to get the hang of his new faith in Christ and of being unselfish. Some people didn't always respond to his kindness, but no matter, Sid's newfound unselfishness had given him a smile and a joy in his heart that he'd never known before.

Sid's father's job ended by August of that summer and they had to move to his next assignment. A few months earlier that move would have made Sid rejoice, but now he was saddened to leave Nit Picky. Before he moved, Sid treated the Nit Picky gang to ice cream floats at the "What-A-Burger".

A few weeks into the new school year, a small package

55

came to Franny's house. It was a gold heart necklace.

The card read: "Never stop being Franny to people like me, for without your concern and love I may have ended my life. But guess what, Franny, I've been elected class president in my new school and they are calling me 'Smiling' Sid. Imagine that."

Love and thanks, Sid.

Chapter

12   Strange Request

In the town of Nit Picky, home of the Fighting Tomcats, summer was a hectic time for a boy named Lonnie Mossberry. Lonnie was the Nit Picky "nerd" before that word was popular. Perhaps Lonnie would have been called a "nerd" because of his constant working, studying, and staying at home on weekends when he reached high school age. Or maybe it was due to the large black-framed glasses that were supported atop his beanpole frame by two extra-large ears. Whatever the case, Lonnie was a good kid, very quiet and busy, but his work kept him out of the main stream of the kids' after school and summer activities.

Lonnie ran his own little business. He did odd jobs year around and yard care from early spring to late fall. His classmates called him "Lawnmower" Lonnie. He wore scrappy clothes for his work, including his brother Joe's hand-me-down ball cap with his name on it. At the service station where Lonnie purchased his mower's gasoline, Sam always called him Joe because of the cap. Lonnie never bothered to correct him.

One particular incident that happened to Lonnie during one of those fast-paced summers began with a phone call to his home. His father answered. The family was about to eat supper.

"Hello. It's for you, Son, I think it's Mrs. Neatyard again," said his somewhat irritated dad.

"Yes, this is Lonnie, how may I help you?" he asked after dashing from the table to the phone. "It did?" he responded. "I'll be right over!"

"Lonnie, you just got in from mowing all day and supper is ready," complained Dad. "Mrs. Neatyard wants you to do what?" Dad asked in amazement.

"Yes, a baby bird has fallen from her purple martin house and she wants me to climb up and put it back before the cats get it," Lonnie said with a grin.

"You've got to be kidding, Son. It's getting late and she lives on the other side of town," moaned his father.

"Dad, Mrs. Neatyard is one of my best customers," said Lonnie. "She hires me to do more work in her yard and house than any other customer I have. If she wants that baby bird back in its nest 15 feet up on a pole, that's what I'll do, it's okay," Lonnie explained. "I'll eat when I get back."

So Lonnie rode across town on his silver-fendered, one speed Shelby bicycle. It had a large clip rack on the front that he used to secure his gas can for mowing. Arriving in time, Lonnie found the tiny featherless bird still alive at the base of the bird-house. Carefully he secured a ladder against the tall pole. When one thinks of the danger of such an act, it must have been the Lord that held the ladder in place.

Slowly, rung by rung, Lonnie edged the wee bird back to its nest. Did the bird survive? He never knew, although from all that he had read, birds usually didn't accept their young with human scent on it.

Mrs. Neatyard thanked Lonnie and paid him for his efforts. He rode back home to a reheated meal, pleased that the task had been accomplished.

The next day Lonnie spotted Franny and stopped to talk to her between mowing jobs. As Lonnie sat telling her about this strange request of Mrs. Neatyard, Franny smiled as she recalled a scripture verse.

Franny quoted the scripture, "Well done, my good servant! ...Because you have been trustworthy in a very small matter, take charge of ten cities." (Luke 19:17) "You know, Lonnie," Franny said, "God is a lot like Mrs. Neatyard. Sometimes He asks us to do what seems small or unimportant. God requests may not make much sense to our friends, relatives, or even to us. But if we're willing to obey, He takes care of the rest." Franny continued, "Does Mrs. Neatyard ever ask you to do larger tasks with more responsibility than that

58

birdhouse job?"

"Why yes, she does," replied Lonnie.

"See, Lonnie, it's like that with God too. If we are faithful to do the small tasks He asks of us, then He can trust us with greater ones," continued Franny. "You had no control over whether that bird lived or not or whether its parents took it back in the nest, that's in God's hands. Your task," explained Franny, "was to simply put the bird back in its nest. That's true with all that God asks of us in life. Obey and leave the results to him."

Franny was right, then she usually was when it came to the Bible. Lonnie thanked her for the sermon and gave her a quarter. "For the offering," he said smiling. Franny chuckled. Lonnie mounted his "silver steed", and with the mower handle in hand, he pulled his bright yellow cutting machine along side as he headed toward his next yard.

In the years that followed Nit Picky, "Lawnmower" Lonnie became a corporation executive for a "small" company by the name of IBM. But he never forgot the lessons he learned as a boy, especially the one of Mrs. Neatyard's strange request.

Chapter

13 Town by the Spring

A challenging assignment in Mr. Dustberger's history class led Franny and the gang to a great discovery. The class was instructed to write a two or three page paper about some historic event that wasn't in their textbook. Since Franny was still fairly new to Nit Picky, she chose to write about its history.

Franny learned about Nit Picky's glorious railroad days. She discovered that Nit Picky once had streetcar tracks down the middle of Main Street. People could ride the few miles to Wicksburg and back for only a nickel. She read where the little town used to employ lamplighters to light the oil street lamps. On a statewide crime spree, gangsters robbed the Nit Picky National Bank in the early 1930s of $10,000. They wounded the bank guard in a shoot-out. Government agents (G-men) captured the mobsters two months later. In the spring of 1937 a flood almost destroyed Nit Picky, forcing the railroad to move its terminal further north, thus nearly bankrupting the waterlogged town. During the summer of 1947, a disastrous train wreck piled train cars and debris all along Rail Street; it took days to clear the wreckage and rebuild the tracks. Franny was told about some huge fires and a tornado or two that had destroyed portions of town. Mayor Bob Dooalot gave her information on political upheavals and scandals that added intrigue to Nit Picky's approximate 117-year history.

But what Franny really wanted to know was how Nit Picky got its name. No one seemed to know. She spent hours at Nit Picky's library, which had once been home to the Church of the All Saints. She talked with some of the oldest members of the community, but no one could explain the name. Franny was pretty certain it wasn't named after a family, because no trace of any folks by the name of Nit Picky could be found. Mr. Dustberger didn't have a clue as to where the name came from and suggested that she try the Wicksburg Library.

"Franny," he said, "the larger library might be of some help to you; it has old newspapers and county records."

Milly Snodgrass agreed to go and help Franny if she would, in turn, help with her project. Franny readily agreed, as she didn't like the idea of going to the Wicksburg Library by herself. After a couple of hours of digging through old papers and books, the girls were just about to give up.

"Franny, I think I've found something!" Milly shouted, only to be shushed by the library lady, Miss Strickland, "Here's something in this old book," Milly whispered. Sure enough, she had found a dusty old book buried in a forgotten corner that held the key to Nit Picky's name--and much more.

In 1835, a wagon loaded with settlers headed west from Pennsylvania happened upon a natural bubbling spring of clear water in the area now known as Nit Picky. The land was suitable for farming. The two rivers only a few miles away provided good transportation and irrigation for fertile grounds.

More settlers followed, and soon there were several log cabins forming the new little community. Before another year had passed, there was a total of seventy folks living around the refreshing spring. Joshua T. McBigstuff decided that the little settlement ought to have a leader and that he was just the fellow to fill the job. So he appointed himself the town's acting boss man. He was accepted, since most of the others didn't want the thankless job.

However, there was one settler by the name of Willy G. McWhiner that was not pleased one little bit with the situation. He felt that an election should be held to select a leader for their unnamed community. McWhiner let it be known that he was just as qualified as "Mr. Bigstuff," as he called him, to serve in that leadership position. Besides, the ten-cent a month salary promised by the community would fit in his pocket just as well as in his opponent's.

The folks living around the spring said the first thing that was needed for their tiny settlement was a name. Every other little burg around them had a name. Suggestions floated about in abundance. Some wanted it to remind people of the first settler, Moorely Flinchkettle; they recommended Mooresville, Moorelyburg, Flinchville, or Kettlestown. Willy McWhiner wanted the name of Rivertown. But McBigstuff argued that it ought to be called Springsburg after the wonderful spring that supplied the town's water.

Another year or so passed, but the growing town still had no name. People of the small settlement would tell passing strangers that they were known only as the town by the spring. Finally, McBigstuff called a town meeting for the sole purpose of discussing a town name. However, it ended in a big fight because no one could agree. Each one tried to out-shout the other. There was complaining and whining by all. After that meeting, hurt feelings abounded in the little town and gossip raged like a wildfire.

As Milly and Franny kept reading, their interest grew with each yellowed page of the old book. They could hardly believe what they read next.

McWhiner told others that McBigstuff had a big a nose and that his ears stuck out. Why, according to McWhiner, McBigstuff was simply too ugly to make a good town leader that they could all be proud of.

McWhiner was quoted as saying, "McBigstuff doesn't have a stitch of decent clothes to wear."

In the meantime, McBigstuff told folks, "McWhiner has sticky fingers around money, and besides, he has never fixed the gate on the town cemetery that he was paid to do."

As the girls continued to read on, they learned that one thing led to another in the little town by the spring until, before long, everybody was quite angry with every body else. Everyone, it seemed, began telling stories on their neighbors. Examples included: "Sarah Church's dresses are too short" and "Wally, the barber, has a scraggly beard and talks too much". Other rumors included: "Edgy Spillwater is always too drunk on Saturday evenings to ride his horse home" and "Lucenda Ruffhouse is so worldly that the church ladies never invite her to tea; everybody knows that she flirts with Edgy in public."

It became so bad that people in the surrounding farms and communities stayed away from the shops in the little town by the spring. Folks in neighboring towns made jokes about the fighting town. The people in the little unnamed town would cross the dirt streets to avoid each other. They would turn their noses up in the air to each other when they met.

Milly and Franny giggled uncontrollably when Milly said the town should have been named "Snootsville." The librarian was fast to shush them again.

Turning another dusty page, the girls read that on September 8, 1839, a fire broke out in McBigstuff's dry-goods store. The store's owner rang the town fire bell and people came running. He was shouting out orders to get buckets and form a line from the spring to his store. McWhiner shouted back at him asking who had appointed him head of the fire department. Edgy Spillwater complained at the size of buckets that folks were bringing; they were either too large or too small. Lucenda Ruffhouse whined that the line of folks to the spring was crooked and not evenly spaced, so she broke ranks to straighten everyone out. Meanwhile, flames were quickly eating McBigstuff's store. The whole scene became a chaotic shouting match. The folks fussed over everything, including the fact that no one had put on their volunteer firemen hats and boots.

Franny and Milly turned the next page to read: "Then a heart-stopping scream was heard from the end of the newly-organized bucket brigade. The spring had stopped flowing!"

The alarm went through the line of folks like a horrible plague. They stood in disbelief while McBigstuff's store became nothing more than a pile of ashes. As if hit by a hot-southwestern wind, the town's folk began to wilt in grief for their lost store and even more for their spring.

It was at that point that the folks noticed him. Dusty from travel, he was dressed in a black suit with long tails and topped with a stovepipe hat that shaded his piercing eyes. He perched atop his sleek-dark steed that was damp from its ride. The wise old circuit preacher Reverend George P. Clearwater III, was paying them a surprise visit--and during the big fire no less.

With his worn black leather Bible clenched in one hand and the reigns of his trusted horse, St. John, in the other, he marveled at the people's predicament. First, he called the people to prayer. Then, with blistering speech, he began to preach to them from atop his stately mount.

"You foolish people," he proclaimed with a passion, "I've watched you and listened to you gripe and complain over these past years. You bicker and fight and tear each other apart and look where it has gotten you! Your store is gone and your spring is dry." He continued, "The Bible says in Matthew 23:24 that there are those who 'strain out a gnat but swallow a camel'.

And that's just what you have done!"

"He was sure fired up!" Franny exclaimed to Milly, only to hear the librarian clear her throat real loud in a 'you two be quiet' tone.

Reading on, the girls picked up where Preacher Clearwater said, "You have been so petty with each other all these years and now it has cost dearly. You're always fighting like a bunch of tomcats," he bellowed!

By now the Rev. Clearwater had the folks' attention and they knew he was right. Franny and Milly both smiled as they thought how it would be for their own Rev. Watchman to preach like that on Sunday.

Preacher Clearwater, with Bible still in hand, continued, "You people have been so busy fussing about the little things, and worrying over unimportant matters, like a town name and a town boss, that you failed to notice how your beloved spring was caving in and blocking its flow. You're nothing but a town of nit-pickers, you're like the Pharisees of Christ's day," fired the Reverend. "The **spring of living water, Jesus,** was right in their midst and they were so concerned over matters of their law and their own well-being that they let Jesus go right past without realizing he was the very Son of God. Now, before I come back to preach in two weeks, come Sunday, I want to see some serious making up and getting right with the Lord and each other." Then the black-suited man of the Lord galloped off in a trail of dust that left them all coughing.

Well the rest, as they say, is history. The book didn't record who made the decision, but from that day in September 1839, to this, the little town by the spring became known as the town of Nit Picky, home of the Fighting Tomcats.

Franny told Mr. Dustberger as she handed in her paper, "It's a shame more people in our little town don't know the reason behind its name. If they did, maybe they'd be a little less nit-picky and a whole lot more like Jesus."

After giving her an A+ on her paper, Mr. Dustberger sent a copy to *The Nit Picky Weekly Tribunal*. The editor placed it on the front page of the next edition.

Chapter

14 You Hafta Spit on the Bait

The old man moseyed over to the stump and sat down. When the Nit Picky gang spotted him, they gathered around to see if he was okay.

"I was just thinking and remembering," he said.

"About what, mister?" the kids asked in chorus.

"Well," he began, "in this little town of Nit Picky where folks know folks and neighbors are often helpful, there once lived a young fellow by the name of 'Lonely' Larry. That's what the kids at school called him. He attended the Nit Picky Grade School just as I suppose you youngins do. Is it still called home of the Fighting Tomcats?" he asked.

"Yes!" shouted the kids with glee.

The old man began to tell the gang the following story.

"Now 'Lonely' wasn't a friendless child or anything like that," said the bearded old man. "He was simply a quiet boy, an only child who was used to being around adults."

"Lonely" would ride his bike for miles with his dog and the blue sky as companions. As a younger child, he'd learned to entertain himself. He would play for hours on end with his toy soldiers under the giant maple trees at his sitter's. His parents both worked, and he'd stay with the white-haired lady until they picked him up in the evening. Larry had learned that most of the time being alone was okay. But to the children, who thought you had to have a bunch of buddies around all the time, Larry seemed a bit strange. Someone called him "Lonely" one day and the nickname stuck.

With a twinkle in his eye, the old fellow said, "Larry wasn't rough and tumble like a lot of fellows his age, nor was he very good at athletic events. Now, that's not to say he couldn't hit a baseball or scuffle now and then. Why there was the time.... well that's another story."

Continuing, the old fellow said, "Living next door to Larry in those days was an old man, 'bout the age I am now. His name was Harvey D.; he loved to fish. Harvey worked on the Gulf Mobile Railroad and had several fingers missing due to work related accidents, but that didn't hinder his hobby one little bit. Quite often when Harvey came in from work, he'd load up his car with his cane fishing poles, tackle, a bucket of minnows, and an old gasoline motor. Then off he'd go to the lake. He had his home-built johnboat secured to a wooden dock that jutted out into the lake several yards.

Now Harvey had watched young Larry grow up from the age of three to be a fellow mature enough to perhaps do some serious fishing. One day he asked the young Larry if he'd like to go fishing with him. Larry jumped at the chance. He seldom was able to go with his dad because he worked long hours and wasn't too interested in fishing. Besides, Larry was itching to try out the tackle box of hooks and sinkers and the like that he had received that past Christmas from a neighbor lady.

Not all boys Larry's age could do serious fishing; they couldn't sit still in the boat for hours on end. They wanted to run

and play or be entertained by others. However, "Lonely" Larry's personality and lifestyle made him a suitable fishing partner for old Harvey D. He soon learned that Larry was a boy who could fish for as long as any grownup. He'd gladly fish until the sun disappeared behind the cypress trees that filled the lake. Harvey took the young boy under his wing and Larry was good help to the aging Harvey with all the fishing gear. They became the best of fishing buddies for years.

Harvey taught Larry how to fish, how to tie his line, how to bait his hook, what bait to try next and how deep to fish. Together they caught a ton of fish in the years that followed, well maybe not a full ton, but a whole lot. Harvey even taught Larry to spit on the bait for better luck. Larry was convinced it worked for they never failed to catch fish even when no one else did.

Summers came and went for Larry and Harvey. Larry grew taller and Harvey grew older. He became more unable to handle the boat and drive his aging car. Larry got a job and didn't have much time to fish. Their days together became but a pleasant memory. Larry eventually went away to school and never lived in Nit Picky again. Harvey died and so did Mrs. D. Their decaying house was torn down. Only memories remained.

As the now-aged Larry talked to the Nit Picky kids, he thought back on his days in Nit Picky, he thought of Harvey D. and how the old fisherman had favored him over all the other neighborhood boys to take fishing. He remembered the many stringers full of fish they had caught. Larry was sure that old Harvey had benefited from his companionship and help, but the kindness to a lanky kid called "Lonely" had never been forgotten after all the years.

Larry stood up and stretched his arthritic joints as he continued talking to Franny, Susy, Lonnie, Phil, Milly, "Clutts", and the rest of the Nit Picky gang who had gathered on the corner of Oak and 3rd streets to hear his story. Larry pointed out where he'd lived so many years ago and where Harvey D.'s house had once stood. The children delighted in the old man's story as they tried their best to imagine him ever being the young boy called "Lonely" Larry.

Before Larry had to leave, he told the boys and girls, "You know that God's word tells us in 1 Thessalonians 5:15 to '…always try to be kind to each other and to everyone else'. That's what I remember most about old Harvey D. He was kind to me as a little boy who wanted to learn how to fish.

"Kids," Larry went on to say, "I'm not in that big a hurry today, and I happen to have a whole trunk full of fishing gear." With a gleam in his eyes he said, "My wife won't care that I have my good shoes on. What do you say we go down the street to Nit Picky Pond and I'll teach you how to spit on the bait to catch the big ones?"

It was a day the kids of Nit Picky were to remember for a long time. Old Larry caught the biggest fish, of course, but they all caught something. "Clutts" caught a mud-filled boot, but he really didn't care, because of the good time he was having.

Days after Larry left Nit Picky, the boys and girls were still talking about Larry's story about Harvey D. They shared with others how Larry had taught them to spit on the bait.

Franny said to the gang, "You see, kindness is not just something you and I are to receive, but it is something we are to give away. That's the lesson Jesus teaches us through folks like Harvey D. and 'Lonely' Larry. In kindness and love Jesus went

69

so far as to give his very life for us that we might have forgiveness of sin. He tells us to pass His kindness on to others."

Continuing, Franny said, "We know that spitting on the bait doesn't bring good luck, but maybe in some way it's symbolic of kindness for a young boy called 'Lonely' Larry and now for us."

Good luck or not, however, the Nit Picky gang grew up always spitting on their fish bait. For, who knew, maybe old Harvey D. was right after all.

Chapter

15   The Camping Trip

Near the town of Nit Picky there was a state park called **Horsehead Lake**. It had that name because, from the air, it looked like the head of a horse. It was the same lake where Harvey D. had taken Larry fishing, many years ago. The lake was home to large-mouth bass, black crappie and thousands of seasonal Canadian Geese. It was also a neat place to camp. It had tall cypress trees that actually grew in the water and snakes that made the trees their home. But snakes shouldn't be discussed when thinking of camping. There's a better tale to tell.

Nick Woodsman or "Neat" Nick as his friends called him, and "Laid Back" Lenny Coolman, were friends of "Clutts" Clinkmyer. These three buddies had planned for weeks to go camping over the Labor Day weekend. It would be their last camping trip for the summer. "Clutts" was responsible for the food, "Laid Back" was in charge of getting transportation, and "Neat" Nick was to secure the tent and supplies.

The trio arrived Friday afternoon, found a secluded site and set up camp. It consisted of a four-man walled tent, a grill to cook over the fire, a few fishing poles, and a lot of snacks. Soon they were into some serious fishing and general tomfoolery until dark. Then they roasted some hot-dogs over the campfire and sat talking about the large snake they had seen that afternoon. Nick said it was a Cottonmouth Moccasin, "Laid Back" thought it to be a King snake, and "Clutts" swore it was a Python. The other two were quick to tell him Pythons didn't live around those parts.

The boys told tall fish-tales that soon became tall ghost stories. They ended up scaring themselves. To finish their evening before dousing the fire, they pigged out on chocolate bars covered with burnt marshmallows smashed between two stale graham crackers. That concoction, along with the stories, was a good combination for heartburn and nightmares.

After the fire was out, the boys realized how dark it was out there. They were used to the streetlights of Nit Picky, and there wasn't even a moon glow to push away the darkness. But they weren't afraid, for after all, they were 8th graders. Besides, there were park rangers to watch out for them. The three boys were like a pack of dogs in a straw pile trying to make their beds in that small tent. At last they had nested, told their last jokes and became as still as dead men in a graveyard. But, wouldn't you know it "Neat" Nick decided he needed one more trip to the outdoor potty before he could go to sleep.

"Would one of you guys go with me to stand watch at the door?" he asked, being a bit fearful of the darkness.

"NOPE!" "NOPE!" responded the two sleepy tent-mates.

So "Neat" Nick took his trusty ten-battery, goose-necked, deluxe-waterproofed, unsinkable-elongated, army-green flashlight and started down the spooky path to the outdoor "john". The dark and curvy path led about 300 yards into the woods. Nick had been gone long enough that both "Clutts" and "Laid Back" had fallen sound asleep. Suddenly they were torn from their dreams by shouts of "HELP! HELP! SAVE ME! HELP!" The two boys almost made a new door in the tent as they both tried to exit at the same time. They were sure that old "Neat" was being eaten alive by the four-foot snake they'd seen earlier.

72

Pausing a moment in the story, one should understand something about the outhouse (outdoor toilet) at their camp sight. It was a small wooden building about five feet wide by four feet deep by seven feet tall. It had four tiny screened holes near the roof on each side and a small pipe on top for ventilation. The bottom edge of the little building fit crudely over a slab of concrete. There were gaps around the bottom edge caused by decaying boards. The roof was made of corrugated metal (that's metal with ruffles). On the door of the skinny structure was painted a quarter-moon symbol; that was so folks knew it was an outhouse. Inside the tiny building were two holes on the wooden bench, which made it possible for two folks to use the bathroom at the same time, if they had a mind to, but few folks ever did.

Now, back to old "Neat" and his bellowing, for he was still screaming bloody murder when the boys arrived.

"That's strange," whispered "Clutts", "there's no light at all coming from the outhouse!"

73

Cautiously, "Laid Back" Lenny threw open the door and jumped back at the same time, while "Clutts" held his flashlight toward the opening. There stood "Neat" in his bright yellow, footed pajamas, pale as a ghost, and shaking like a tree in a windstorm. He was pointing to the 2nd of the two holes on the wooden bench seat.

Laughter split the sides of "Clutts" and "Laid Back". It wasn't a snake after all. "Neat", with all his preciseness and neatness, had accidentally knocked his super-deluxe flashlight down the 2nd hole and into the "yucky" mess below. The good news was that the deluxe flashlight floated! "Neat" had stood in darkness all that time, while the lower portion of the "john" had had plenty of light. Being church kids, the song *LET YOUR LOWER LIGHTS BE BURNING* popped into the minds of the two would-be rescuers. Before long they had the nervous "Neat" singing and laughing too. One could only wonder what the forest creatures thought about that late-night ruckus.

The following Tuesday when the boys told Franny about their venturesome weekend, she was not only quick to laugh, but also to put a spiritual truth to it all, she was good at that. She quoted Matthew 5:16: "...let your Light shine before men, that they may see your good deeds and praise your Father in heaven."

Franny told them, "Perhaps the Lord wanted to teach us that we should never think too highly of ourselves lest we goof-up and knock our lights down the 'john'." She went on to say, "The experience should show us how we are never to think ourselves too good to shine the light of Jesus among the down and outcast, the undesirables, the unloved, those that the world has given up on. They need to see the light of Jesus too. His light shines even in the worst of places. Even though not all that see his light will receive it, we are still to let the light of Jesus shine through us in a sin-darkened world."

The kids understood what Franny meant because her spiritual light had brightened up good-old Nit Picky Grade School, home of the Fighting Tomcats.

Eventually "Neat" Nick grew up to become a noted archaeologist. But it was said that he never went into dark places without an extra flashlight.

Chapter

16 A Sad Day in Nit Picky

There was one Monday in Nit Picky, home of the Fighting Tomcats, that it felt as if someone had suddenly pulled

the plug on the sun. The emotional darkness that enveloped the little grade school resembled a king-size quilt being spread over a twin-size bed. Mr. Gravity Moore, the beloved science teacher, had just spoken to the school assembly and had taken his seat. Some of the Nit Picky gang covered their mouths with their hands, some wiped tears from their eyes, some just sat there not knowing what to do. Their teacher, Mr. Moore had just informed them that he and his family were moving to Kansas in two weeks and that this would be his last week at school. He explained to them that the school board and Principal Straightshooter had already secured his replacement, Mr. Fulcrum.

Teacher Moore had taught the Nit Picky gang science from their sixth grade on. He had helped them to actually enjoy learning about the world in which they lived. Mr. Moore had won the hearts of the kids. He had taught them by allowing them to have hands-on experiences. But perhaps his best qualities were his love and care for the children. They in return, loved and respected him and didn't want him to leave.

In his speech, Mr. Moore explained that his aging mother and father were in poor health and needed his help; he was their only child. A teaching job had opened in Callsville, Kansas, and he felt it was God's will that he accept the position. Mr. Moore explained that for a science teacher position to open in the middle of the school year that close to his parents was not an accident. He told them that the Lord had to have been involved. Mr. Moore knew that most of the children would understand his talk about God because many of them went to church in Nit Picky. Some attended where he and his family belonged.

"Seenit-Donethat" Susy took the news particularly hard. One might recall that it was Mr. Moore who had rescued her in the Chicago museum from the would-be kidnapper. Over the next few days, Susy cried until her "eye-wells" went dry. She couldn't seem to get a grip on her feelings. Gale Griper was also very sad. After all, it had been Mr. Moore along with Mrs. Playwright that had led the kids and others to help Gale's family through some difficult and needy days. Franny could sympathize with the pain that her friends were experiencing and knew that they needed some extra love and encouragement.

Franny knocked on Susy's door early Saturday morning, the day the Moore's were to leave town. Gale was already there. Franny had prayed that the Lord would help her understand and be of help to Susy, Gale, and the rest of the Nit Picky gang. When Franny had done her Bible readings the night before, she read in the Old Testament, "Now Joshua son of Nun was filled with the spirit of wisdom because **Moses had laid his hands on him**...." (Deuteronomy 34:9a) Franny told Susy and Gale how that verse spoke of a time when Moses was about to die. He would go to heaven with God while Joshua would be left to lead the people of Israel into the Promised Land.

Franny said, "As I read that verse, the Lord showed me a meaning of Moses laying his hands on Joshua. It means that

76

Moses had been Joshua's teacher for all those years in the desert and during that time the Lord had been touching his life through Moses. His instruction would help Joshua face the trials of a new land." Franny went on to say, "Joshua, must have been broken hearted to see Moses leave just like we are to see Mr. Moore go. But Joshua knew, as we do, that life hurts sometimes and that times of change come to all." Franny reminded the girls that God had helped them through sad times in the past and would no doubt help them again. God led Franny that day to show Susy, Gale, and the rest of the kids how the influence and help Mr. Moore had been in their lives wouldn't leave when he moved. It would always be a part of them.

"I realize now," Franny said to her friends, "Mr. Moore will not only be a part of our lives forever, but you and I and the entire gang will always be a part of his life, too." Franny dried her eyes as she reassured the girls, "Friendships, loves, and the lessons learned from others are not things that are packed in a suitcase and put on a truck when moving time comes. They are the things that are left behind in one's heart and mind. Just as the Lord took Moses to a new land, God is moving Mr. Moore to a new place of service." Franny continued, "If God can take Mr. Moore away, He can also see that the new science teacher, Mr. Fulcrum, will continue to help us."

"But Franny," Susy exclaimed, "no one will ever be like Mr. Moore! He was the best!"

Franny, in a partial laugh, explained, "You're right, Susy, and the one taking his place shouldn't be expected to be just like him. As God helped us through Mr. Moore, God can and will help us in different ways through our new teacher."

"But what if I like this new fellow," asked Gale, "would I be disloyal to Mr. Moore's memory?"

"Heavens no!" Franny exclaimed. "In fact, I believe it would be a tribute and honor to Mr. Moore for us to love and learn from the new teacher like we did from him. Let's go ask him now. It's almost time for all the gang to meet at his house to say good bye."

The Moore family was thrilled to see the rag-tag Nit

Picky gang of kids that came to see them off.   Mr. Moore assured Franny and the gang that he'd be quite happy if they liked their new teacher and continued to learn from him.

The doors on the moving van closed, the truck's engine puffed black smoke from its exhaust as it gave a jolt and rolled away.   The time for the Moore's to pile into their old station wagon and head west had arrived.

Franny stepped forward and handed Mr. Moore a box about the size of a large shoebox.   It was crudely wrapped with the newspaper comic section.   "ALLEY-OOP" and his dinosaur were showing on the top of the package; the kids knew this was Mr. Moore's favorite comic strip.   He quickly opened the package as his wife and two children looked on. Inside he found items signed by the kids.   There was a laminated four-leafed clover from "Lawnmower" Lonnie, a picture and news article of "Seenit-Donethat" Susy at the Chicago museum, and a baseball cap from "Haughty" Hank that he had received at a St. Louis Cardinal's game.   Also, he found a picture of "Neat" Nick, "Laid Back" Coolman, and "Clutts" in front of their famous outhouse, and a tiny handmade motor that had won first prize for "Perfect" Phil at the science fair.   Mr. Moore shed a tear as he picked up the blue ribbon won by "Poor Boy" Pete Ridder at the soapbox derby, and the cracked bicycle reflector from "Clutts" Clinkmyer's historic crash on "THE HILL". Perhaps what touched Mr. Moore the most was found at the bottom of the box; it was a small New Testament that was worn and marked. It had Franny's name and a date printed inside the front cover. Her note simply said, "Take this Bible, I have another now, but this one was used to lead me to Jesus. Love Franny."

The entire box was filled with the kids' special gifts for Mr. Moore to remember them. The kids didn't have much money and wouldn't have known what to get him anyway, so they had decided to give him items dear to their hearts.

The children learned that day that sacrificial love could even make a grown man cry. But then that was just another lesson from God through Mr. Moore.

Years and teachers were to come and go in the lives of the Nit Picky kids. The gang of friends would all eventually grow up and go their separate ways to life's new adventures. However, the lessons they learned from Mr. Moore, Mrs. Playwright, Mr. Divisor, Principal Straightshooter, and their many other teachers, families, and friends would remain a part of their hearts and lives forever.

Chapter

17 Mayhem at the City Dump

It was the summer of '62 in the little town of Nit Picky, home of the Fighting Tomcats, and "Fearless" Frank was bored. His thoughts turned to the barbershop stories that he'd heard concerning the awful place across the railroad tracks. Frank's youthful spirit was peaked with curiosity. Those "tall tales" told by the barber had always made him wonder. He wasn't sure if the stories were true or if they were simply used to scare boys like him into sitting still. Everyone knew the barber wasn't particularly fond of cutting kids' hair. However, the stories did sound believable and something that a fearless young man, like himself, should check out. Frank's parents had warned him never ever go across the tracks, especially by himself.

"But, I'm going to be an eight grader in the fall! I'm big enough to take care of myself!" Frank exclaimed to himself.

Jumping on his trusty Road-Buster bicycle, Frank took his leather-covered transistor radio and army surplus canteen. He strapped his reliable "Red Rider" BB gun across the handle bars as he headed for that forbidden place. Old "Fearless" was soon out of sight as he wound around the narrow cinder-covered path that led to what all the town folk called, **the dump**. The dense brush and trees that hid Nit Picky from the dump now concealed Frank from Nit Picky. Almost invisible too, in that tangled wilderness, were the rat-infested foundations of the decayed buildings of Nit Picky's past railroad days.

Black smoke could be seen wafting above the brush as "Fearless" neared the dump. A pungent odor filled his nostrils as he panted to make "old silver" (that's what he called his bicycle) travel the road that had become nothing more that a dusty path. "Fearless" rounded the last curve to find himself staring at a vast mountain of junk. Broken glass, rusted cans, decayed cloth and paper, torn automobile seats, treadless tires, busted tubs and sinks, and rotting garbage made up that massive mess.

Undaunted by the sights and smells, "Fearless" determined even more to explore the eerie burning pile of junk. Cocking his fully loaded BB gun, he wandered in and out, over and around Nit Picky's dark side. Without warning, Frank's foot slipped on a dusty old car hood and he fell, striking his leg on a chunk of concrete. His canteen wheeled off landing out of reach. His leg was bent unnaturally and wouldn't move as pain pounded from its tangled form. But Frank had managed to hang onto his gun. That proved to be a lifesaver against the possum-sized rats that looked on with curiosity at this heap of humanity that was suddenly hurled among them.

How long would his BBs last, in fact, how long would he last in the scorching sun with no water? The barber's stories had been true all right, and the warnings from Frank's parents should have been listened to. "Hadn't it been just last Sunday, when the Reverend McDifference had preached on a place called Hell?" thought Frank. And now he felt as if he had found it. The preacher had read from the Bible: "And the devil, who deceived them, was thrown into the lake of burning sulfur, where the beast and the false prophet had been thrown. They will be tormented day and night forever and ever." (Rev. 20:10)

The glaring summer heat turned Frank's mouth into a sandy beach as sweat dripped from his chin. The nauseating odors of burning garbage removed the last trace of "fearlessness" from Frank. He was angry with himself for disobeying his parents. The fear of never seeing them again hovered over Frank like the smoke that was enfolding him. The frightened boy began to cry; he called on the Lord to save him from that horrible mess. His consciousness faded, as his gun slid out of reach.

Frank didn't know whether he was dreaming or losing touch with his senses, but he was sure that he'd heard his name being called out. There it was again. In fact, he was hearing his name from several voices. Then the voices and bodies came into focus at the top of the old car hood; it was Franny, Phil, Milly, "Clutts", and most of the Nit Picky gang.

The kids had dropped by Frank's to see if he wanted to join them for ice cream at Charlie's Market. Frank's neighbor, Mrs. I. C. Everything, was sitting on her porch swing when the gang knocked on Frank's door. She quickly told them, "Frank's not home, no one is there." Then she added, "As I was driving into Nit Picky this morning from my shopping trip to Wicksburg, I saw a boy that looked a lot like Frank headed off the highway toward the dump. But his folks have told him never to go there." However, her last words about "never to go there" were lost to the kids as they clattered their bicycles westward.

Franny let out a shriek when she saw Frank's condition and the dead rats nearby. Phil choked on the smoke as he grabbed the unused canteen. He gave Frank what seemed to be a spring of water from heaven itself. "Clutts" Clinkmyer made dust with his bicycle as he tore for town and the much needed help. Milly and some of the others, pinching their noses, just kept saying how much it stank out there.

Sid asked Frank, "What are you doing here?"

"Playing the fool," Frank said, "playing the fool." He told Franny and friends about his ordeal and the similarities to the place called hell as described by Rev. McDifference. "Can you imagine," said Frank, "what it would be like to live in a place like this for ever and ever with no hope of ever seeing Jesus or your loved ones?"

Franny reminded Frank and the gang that the Bible verses Sunday had included one in Revelations 1:18 where Jesus said, "I am the Living One; I was dead, and behold I am alive forever and ever! And I hold the keys of death and Hades." "The good news," said Franny, "is that Jesus controls the keys of both heaven and hell. And when we admit we are sinners, believe in our hearts that Jesus is God's son, and commit our lives to Him, we receive Jesus' promise that we will never have to live in the place called hell that was made for the Devil and his followers."

Red lights flashed, sirens blared, and dust flew as help arrived to take Frank from the clutches of Nit Picky's little taste of "Hades". Frank was glad to leave, but even more than that, he rejoiced that because of Jesus in his heart he'd never have to face the real place.

Frank promised that when he got off his crutches and being grounded, he wouldn't venture into forbidden places again. He didn't have to be told to sit still in the barber chair either.

83

Chapter

18   "Greedy" Gerty

Many years ago in the little town of Nit Picky, home of the Fighting Tomcats, Easter arrived as a rite of spring with all of its joyous celebration. It's on one particular Easter that we remember yet another of the old Nit Picky troop; the children called her "Greedy" Gerty. Through her years at the grade school, Gerty had built up quite a reputation for being stingy. She'd never share her lunch with anyone who had none. At recess and in class she had earned the name "Greedy" because she wouldn't allow others to borrow or use her crayons or other learning tools or playthings. This was true even when she wasn't using the requested items or had more than she needed.

At home Gerty was no different; when forced to share by her parents, she was quick to take the most cookies, the biggest piece of pie, or the largest portion of a candy bar. "Tattling" Ted, her younger brother by fourteen months, told the gang how he'd even seen "Greedy" snatch the waitress's tips from the tables in Joanna's Restaurant. The poor lady would become so angry over the "tight-wad" customers that her face would turn red. Ted also reported that during one summer when they were visiting their grandmother's house, his selfish sister ate the last piece of watermelon. Ted said, "Gerty knew that our p-o-o-r old grandmother had saved it for her afternoon snack. Besides," Ted went on to say, "Gerty had already eaten half of the melon."

But perhaps Milly Snodgrass told the most condemning story concerning "Greedy". She recalled the details of an Easter egg hunt that happened when she and Gerty were in the fourth grade. Gerty simply showed up at the egg hunt that was being held at the **All Right Church of the Saved**, pastored by the Rev.

Bewildered. Milly's mom had reluctantly agreed to help some of the neighborhood mothers host the party. She insisted that Milly go with her. Even though Milly could have participated, she was shy and so near the age limit that she refused to join in.

"As it turned out, Gerty was the oldest and the biggest of all the children attending the party," Milly said. "None of the other children were a match for her. 'Greedy' scooped up those eggs like a 'wild woman'. She left so few eggs that when the hunt ended most of the kids had nothing in their baskets but air. The dear ladies of the church encouraged Gerty to share her huge find, but she stubbornly refused." Milly concluded.

"Greedy" said quite forcefully, "I found 'em' and I'm going to keep 'em'!"

The truth was, Gerty didn't even like boiled eggs, colored or not. When her mother found out, as mother always seem to do, she was sad and very disappointed at her daughter's behavior. In love, her mom spanked her for her greediness. Gerty was told that she would never get to attend another Easter egg hunt.

"Tattling" Ted jumped in like he normally did, and said, "That spanking didn't phase my big sister one little bit. She'd figured that she would get 'whooped' and had slipped some extra padding down her bottom. I threatened to tell on her, but she promised to 'whoop' me if I did and she could, so I didn't."

The Bible teaches in Galatians 6:7 that we reap what we sow, and so it was for Gerty. In her case it happened at good old Nit Picky Grade School, home of the Fighting Tomcats, on the last day before Easter break of her seventh grade.

The Social Studies teacher, Mrs. Kindheart had prepared each of her students an Easter treat. The students were too old for Easter baskets, they said, so Mrs. Kindheart renamed her treats "surprise boxes". Inside each box were homemade goodies, store-bought candies, and a small present for each child. "Clutts" got his, Phil and Milly got theirs, and Franny had received hers and so it went.

"Land-sakes!" exclaimed the red-faced teacher. "I've forgotten Gerty's Easter box, and most of it won't be any good after our vacation. I'm so sorry Gerty," said Mrs. Kindheart with a quivering-sad voice.

"Greedy" Gerty, in one big bag of emotions, was hurt, angry, sad, and embarrassed. She turned away from the class and toward the windows so they wouldn't see the tears welling up in her eyes. Her spirit was crushed. "How could she forget me?" Gerty questioned. "How? Why me?"

Then, just as the Lord often does, He impressed a thought in her mind. "Gerty, now you know how it feels to be left out; remember that Easter egg hunt a few years ago? You are greedy and don't share." The scripture Rev. Bewildered had read Sunday echoed in Gerty's heart, "Then *Jesus* said, 'Watch out! Be on your guard against all kinds of greed; a man's life does not consist in the abundance of his possessions." (Luke 12:15)

Gerty felt alone and empty as she heard the others open their "surprise boxes" and claim the goodies. As she stared out the window, she felt remorse over her past behavior. She realized how selfish she had been. Gerty didn't dare dream that anyone would share with her; after all, she knew how she had treated her classmates in similar situations. Now she was the one with the "air-filled basket".

Amid all the class commotion, Gerty felt a tap on her shoulder. She turned to find Mrs. Kindheart stooping over and looking her square in the eye. There was a smile on the teacher's face. With joy in her voice, Mrs. Kindheart said, "Gerty, each of your classmates, under Franny's leading, have taken one thing from their own boxes to make an Easter surprise for you. One person even gave you their gift item." She added, "They didn't feel right not sharing with you."

Franny, who never missed a chance to speak up for Jesus, said, "How could we not share with you at Easter, which is the celebration of the gift of life that Christ offers to all who will believe and trust in Him. Happy Easter, Gerty." The whole class cheered, especially Mrs. Kindheart, in the joy of the moment,

"Happy Easter back," said Gerty with a sheepish grin forming on her tear-streaked face.

Yes, that was the Easter that "Greedy" learned what it felt like to be left out and to be let back in again. It took effort, but with the Lord's help and friends like Franny, Milly, and the gang, Gerty came to be known as "Gracious" Gerty.

In the years that followed, Gerty went on to college and become a grade school teacher. She too gave her children Easter "surprise boxes". But Gerty always made sure there were extras so that no one was ever missed.

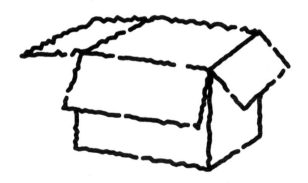

Chapter

19   Odor in Nit Picky

It was late October in Nit Picky, home of the Fighting Tomcats. Excitement electrified the air at the Nit Picky Grade School as the annual Fall Festival approached. Children were pairing up in the eighth grade class in preparation for the activities. Only their class was allowed to operate the games that included fishing, shoot the duck, smack the clown, and cakewalk. All the proceeds from the games and concessions went to purchase new items for the school. The hope was that they would earn enough money that year to purchase a new score board for their small gym.   The board was to have a mean looking, bigger-than-life Fighting Tomcat painted in the center. Plans were that the scoreboard would also make the sound of a fighting cat each time the Nit Picky team scored.

Everyone in the class was pretty well paired up for the games except for "No Time" Tommy. No one, but no one, wanted to be his partner. His homeroom math teacher, Mr. Stillworth, could understand the class, but was concerned as to what he could do. Tommy had grown up on what folks called the wrong side of the tracks, not too far from the city dump. His mother had run off with another man leaving the six-year old Tommy with his dad and four older siblings. His dad tried hard enough to raise the kids, but his long hours on the railroad left little time for them. You might say that "No Time" Tommy pretty much raised himself.

Perhaps it was more that year than ever before, that the kids of the eighth grade noticed Tommy. He took no time to do things like take a bath, brush his "yellow" teeth, comb his wild hair, or clean the ton of dirt from under his fingernails. He also had no time to say please or thank you, or to help others. "No Time" simply had no time for anything except getting dirtier, smellier, and more annoying. One day "No Time" rushed through the door ahead of Susy, who just happened to be carrying a large cake. He allowed the door to flop back in her face. The red-faced Susy had cake from head to toe. Kids claimed that the icing melted under the heat of her anger. The class was terribly upset also because the cake was for their party.

It became so bad with "No Time" Tommy that word had it that even the Nit Picky cats and dogs were crossing to the other side of the street to pass him. You might say Tommy had become isolated from the world. Even his brother and three sisters refused to eat at the same time he did. Tommy looked, acted, and smelled bad, **really, really bad**.

One day, with the Fall Festival just days away and no one wanting to work with him, he spotted "Flawed" Franny sitting on a bench under a maple tree on the play ground. She was enjoying the beauty of the fall colors. Since it was unusual to find Franny without a crowd of friends around her, Tommy grabbed the chance to sit down by her. As nice as Franny was, she still thanked the Lord that she'd finished her lunch before "No Time" had plopped down by her. She never let "No Time" see her turning away occasionally to gasp a fresh breath.

"Franny", Tommy began, "what's wrong with me? No one will be my partner at the carnival and this is the only year we get to do the games."

"Tommy," said Franny, "let me tell you a story from God's word. It's about two men who were building houses. One was wise and one was foolish. The wise one was careful not to neglect all that he needed to do to make his house strong; he built it on the solid rock. The second man was neglectful and

89

had no time for such effort so he built his house on sand because it was the easy way to go." (Matthew 7:24-27)

"What happened to them?" asked Tommy.

"What do you think?" queried Franny. "A storm came and both men ran for the shelter of their houses. The wise one was safe and snug in his house on the rock, but the foolish fellow's house washed out to sea," continued Franny.

"But what's that got to do with me and the festival games," Tommy questioned.

"Tommy," began Franny, "I want to be your friend and sometimes friends have to tell friends things that are hard to take." Going on she said, "Tommy, you smell bad. You're like the man who built on the sand. You don't put out the effort to do the things that will encourage people to like you. You need to take time for Jesus, to clean up, and to be kind to others."

"No Time" looked down as his tears disappeared into the sand below the bench. "Franny, you're right, you know," Tommy began, "You're the only one who has had the courage to be honest with me. I do stink in many ways; I guess I just didn't notice it before. Do you think I can change?" he asked.

"Sure," said Franny, "with the Lord's help all things are possible. We can all change. I tell you what, if you'll take a bath and put on the clean clothes that I know your dad provides for you, I'll be your partner in the toss and hoop game."

"Will you, Franny, honest?" he asked with surprise in his voice. His eyes brightened at the idea of being Franny's partner.

"Yes," Franny said as she gulped for another breath of fresh air. "Now, stop being a 'No Time' Tommy and let Jesus help you build your life on the rock, a clean rock."

The only catch to this story came the next day. No one recognized the cleaned-up boy until he exclaimed, "It's me, 'Tommy.'" The entire class, including Mr. Stillworth and Tommy burst into a **"sweet smelling"** laughter. And, oh yes, that year the carnival was the best ever; the Fighting Tomcats got their new score board that growled with every home score. (See the title page.)

Chapter

20 Nit Picky's Secret Room

One fall day in mid October, "Flawed" Franny, "Perfect" Phil and the rest of the Nit Picky bunch were summoned to the principal's office to see Mr. Straightshooter. No, they weren't in trouble; the principal had selected them for an important task. He had chosen them because they were eighth-graders and seemed to be trustworthy and brave.

"Kids," he began, "the other day I tried to go into the room under the bleachers that is seldom used. I was shocked at how cluttered and dirty it was. I realized why no one ever goes in there; I couldn't go in more than five feet or so. We could use that room and I wondered if you kids would be willing to come Saturday and clean it out. You can toss anything that isn't important. There will be a meal coupon to the 'What-A-Burger' for each of your group that helps. Miss Franny, I'm placing you in charge," he concluded.

The gang felt honored to be selected and was excited about the coupons, that is until they remembered the stories about that area under the bleachers, known to all as the "secret room". Since Franny was a transplant to Nit Picky, she really hadn't heard too much about that mysterious room. However, "Freaky" Freddie was quick to fill her in. "Freaky" was noted for his excessive worry over the simplest matters.

According to Mr. "Fast-Cat," the Nit Picky school bus driver and custodian, nearly fifty-five years ago a man known to all as "One-Armed" Jack had lived in the little town of Nit Picky. Legend had it that Jack was an escaped convict who had been serving time in prison for kidnapping and train robbery. "One-Armed" was a mean villain who supposedly lost his arm during one of his many train robberies. The story was that when he escaped from prison he had shot a school janitor and stole his key to the newly built Nit Picky grade school. Jack supposedly had stored his loot somewhere locally and made his hideout under the school bleachers with a secret passageway for escape.

Mr. "Fast-Cat" would grin mischievously as he told that old "One-Armed" was known to hate children. Mr. "Fast-Cat" always expounded with great emotion and suspense to the kids that children who had misbehaved in school and especially on his own bus had strangely disappeared, never to be heard from again. The jolly, but sly, old bus driver/custodian always made it clear that no one ever captured or found the body of "One-Armed" Jack. The story was never concluded before Mr. "Fast-Cat" added that, sometimes at midnight, when he was all alone sweeping the gym floor, he'd hear terrifying cries and the rattling of bones coming from the "secret room".

"Not too long ago," Mr. "Fast-Cat" would exclaim, "I saw a shad-o-w-y figure of a one-armed man slither through the dimly lighted locker room, headed straight for the secret room. Scared me so bad that I had to stop work the rest of the night." Mr. "Fast-Cat" would slap his knee and laugh a hearty laugh.

"Well," said Franny, "with a story like that no wonder

92

Mr. Straightshooter chose us eighth graders for this job. No lower grader would dare go near that room. I believe Mr. 'Fast-Cat' has a wild imagination and his own method of getting children to behave on the bus," Franny added. "I don't believe in spooks, do you?" she asked the rest of the gang.

"No-o-o-o, n-o-t us," stuttered the kids with a tone of forced bravery.

"I know that there is no such person as 'One-Armed' Jack," said "Fearless " Frank , "you can count me in."

"Me, too!" exclaimed "Clutts" Clinkmyer.

"And me three," said Milly Snodgrass.

After several others joined the clean-up crew, the gang heard one negative voice from the back of the group.

"Not me," said "Neat" Nick, " I can't stand **dark places**."

Early Saturday morning, the gang began to explore and clean that mysterious "secret room". By the way, the room had nooks and bends in it as the bleachers went around the end of the gym; a person couldn't see the whole room from the entrance door. There was so much junk and dirt and cobwebs in that room, that the gang just knew that Mr. "Fast-Cat" had to have been telling a "tall tale"; or was he?

The lighting in the stuffy room wasn't the best either, and Milly screamed when she backed into a skeleton, knocking it over into a heap of bones on the floor. It turned out to be a high school biology class leftover. Funny though, one of its bony arms was missing.

Even "Fearless" Frank let out a yelp when a mouse shot across a support beam past his nose. "Paranoid" Pauline checked every spider to see if it had a red spot on its belly; she was sure some black widow spider would eat them alive. "Clutts" Clinkmyer, when not stumbling and bumbling over old desks, faded pictures and maps, metal files, play props including a suit of armor, and stacks of books, made it his official duty to clear out the cobwebs. "Clutts" loved rolling the webs on the end of the broken yardstick he had found. He was pretending it was his torch and he a great cave explorer.

It was afternoon when, from back in the far corner of the

musty old room, they saw it. An aged chest with a huge clasp and rusty hinges sat covered with dust. The excited kids were certain they had found the lost treasure from "One-Armed" Jack's train robberies, that is, of course, if he was for real.

Carefully they slid the chest into a better light. "Perfect" Phil, taking a deep breath, blew the dust from the lid. Several rounds of sneezes followed. When the dust settled, the kids read the note on the lid. It was marked in huge letters, IMPORTANT STUFF, DO NOT DESTROY. A sigh of disappointment ebbed from the group as they found no gold or jewels when the chest's lid was raised. What they found was junk, just more junk. They found a ball of string, a rubber band ball, a ball of tinfoil, some old license plates, and some cracked dishes. They pulled out some old newspapers, letters, some ancient books and a broken globe. Oh yes, they found a bag or two of marbles and a cracked paddle. Franny was the first to start laughing, and then the rest began to see the humor in it all. The lid was marked "important stuff", but the chest contained nothing but junk, worthless, good-for-nothing stuff.

With their day's work finished, the Nit Picky gang filed into Mr. Straightshooter's office for their "What-A-Burger" coupons. The secret room was usable again.

"Thanks, kids," he said, "now we can store some **important stuff** in the extra space you've made today." The gang burst out laughing, leaving the principal wondering what he'd said that was so funny.

Gathering around a large table at the hamburger joint, the kids relived the day's adventure. Franny told the group how that old chest of junk had reminded her of a verse in the Bible that says, "Do not store up for yourselves treasures on earth, where moth and rust destroy, and where thieves break in and steal. But store up for yourselves treasures in heaven, where moth and rust do not destroy, and where thieves do not break in and steal. For where your treasure is, there your heart will be also." (Matthew 6:19-21) Franny said, "That old chest is like a lot of people's lives, just full of stuff they think is real important, when really it's nothing but junk. For lasting treasures, one should place

94

things like God's salvation, love, joy, peace, hope, grace, and kindness into their lives. These are things that no one can steal from you. These are the important things that last forever."

"Oh, Franny," Phil laughed, "you always see some Godly truth, no matter what we are doing, but that's why we love you so much. Now stop preaching and eat your burger, you deserve it after today's work."

"By the way," asked 'Freaky', "what do you all make of this old shirt I saved from the secret room? It was near the skeleton; **it only has one sleeve!**"

The Gang's eyelids rolled up and their mouths dropped open, but no words came out.

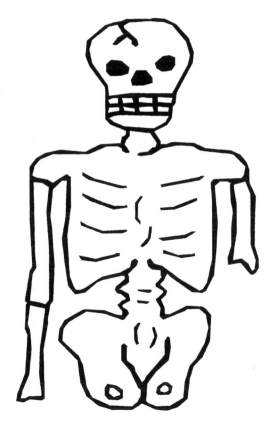

Chapter

21   **The Lost Ring**

It was Christmas time in the little town of Nit Picky, home of the Fighting Tomcats. The kids at good old Nit Picky Grade School would soon learn of yet another serious flaw to a person's character and how its sinful evil could damage the life of another. The gang would not quickly forget, especially Gidget.

This story actually began the previous Christmas when "Clutts" Clinkmyer had received a gold ring from his parents for his Christmas surprise. It had black onyx with a large fancy "C" on the top and his initials were engraved on the inside of the band. "Clutts" had never had a ring before, and, to say the least, he was very proud of it. He was the envy of his friends.

Over that holiday break, "Clutts" had seen many of his classmates, and in a small town like Nit Picky, word about the ring spread quickly. One must remember that as youngsters, the Nit Picky kids weren't very good at estimating what things really cost. The rumor was that the Clinkmyer's had borrowed money on their house to buy "Clutts" the gold ring. The word going around was that the ring had cost his parents nearly $1,000.00. None other than "Gossipy" Gidget had started that story. She had attended all seven grades with "Clutts" and the gang and was known quite well for her wagging tongue.

Inspite of the excitement over the ring, the Clinkmyer's Christmas was marred that year. About five days after Christmas, Grandmother's ceiling fell with a terrible crash onto her kitchen table, chairs, and floor. Fortunately she was not home at the time. The old house that she rented became even worse with the horrible mess made by the fallen ceiling. There was dirt, soot, and plaster everywhere. Since "Clutts" lived close and was accustomed to helping his grandmother, he pitched right in to help her take down the Christmas tree before more dust would be made in the clean up process. The cleaning and repairs took several days. In fact, school had begun again before Grandma's house was livable and "Clutts'" routine was back to normal again. The excitement of his Christmas ring had been forgotten in all the flurry of activities at Grandma's place.

"Gossipy" Gidget caught up with "Clutts" on their first day back in school and begged to see the Christmas ring she'd heard, and talked, so much about.

"Sure," said "Clutts" as he stuck his hand out. "AWH! It's gone!" exclaimed "Clutts", quickly feeling his pockets to see if it was there; it wasn't.

Gidget's eyes sparkled as she saw a real "juicy" story in this unexpected development. "Clutts" panicked. His folks would be heartbroken. He felt irresponsible in his lack of care for such a valuable gift. The search for the ring went on for days, then weeks, but it was gone, gone forever; Clinkmyer was crushed over its loss. The sad boy lost all hope of ever finding his prized ring.

"Maybe I really am nothing more than a klutz, after all," he said to himself.

In the mean time, "Gossipy" Gidget had been busy in her favorite hobby, gossip. It seemed that she took delight in stirring up trouble. She appeared to actually enjoy passing on bad stories about others. In Gidget's mind, she was quick to figure out what had happened to Clinkmyer's expensive ring.   There was a new boy in their class after the Christmas break.   His name was Harold.   The kids had quickly nicknamed him "Hapless" Harold because the shabbily dressed little fellow seemed so unhappy all the time. Well, Miss Gidget had decided that Harold must be a thief and that he had taken "Clutts's" ring during their first morning back in school. She reasoned that he could have easily snitched the ring during the boy's PE class with Coach Bradshaw. She knew "Clutts" was the kind of fellow who would remove the ring before playing the rough games. Gidget assumed that, because Harold was such quiet boy, dressed so poorly, and looked to her like a thief, he must be one.

"Yep! That was it," decided Gidget, and what she decided became the truth as far as she was concerned. "After all, who else could have stolen the valuable ring? We know everyone else in school," she said to all that'd listen.

The rumor spread like the flames on a dry Christmas tree. And, as one might have guessed, Harold was treated as if he had some terrible disease. No one wanted anything to do with a thief. Harold became even more hapless in his appearance. That was the way it went, with Gidget feeding the gossip mills for months, through the summer vacation, and right into the following school year. She just wouldn't let it rest. It was so bad that "Hapless" Harold wished he could move away or die and be laid to rest in peace.

The months fled and Christmas was upon the Nit Picky gang once again. "Clutts", as part of his normal pre-Christmas activity, bought a small tree for his beloved grandmother. He saved money all year for this annual ritual. "Clutts" knew that she wouldn't buy one for herself. He set it up and began to put on the decorations. Some still had to be wiped off from the ceiling dust of the year before. He hoped that such a mess would never happen again.

As "Clutts" reached the bottom of the ornaments box, he noticed something shiny in with the decorations and stuff. "Wow! Glory be! Man! Super! Thank you, Jesus! Here's my ring!" he shouted as he danced around the room. It had evidently slid off his cold finger in the rush to put the ornaments away the previous year. Grandmother's place had been without heat in most of the house because the fallen ceiling had collapsed the pipe on the coal stove. In fact, it had been so cold and messy that Grandma had moved in with "Clutts" and the family during the remodeling. "That's it," he reasoned, "the cold shriveled my fingers so much that the ring came off without my noticing."

The phones began to ring and the tongues wagged in Nit Picky that day and evening concerning the truth about "Clutts'" missing ring. But what about "Hapless" Harold, the supposed thief, the fellow that everyone had treated like dirt for all those past months, how did he feel? And "Gossipy" Gidget, who, by the way, attended church and had been taught about the evil of gossiping, how did she react? Well, Gidget was very ashamed of what she had done to Harold. She apologized to him before the entire class for not only judging him, but for telling things about him that weren't true. She tearfully promised never again to gossip. Franny said that the Bible teaches: "Do not go about spreading slander among your people. Do not do anything that endangers your neighbor's life. I am the LORD." (Leviticus 19:16) Franny depended on God's word and encouraged the class do likewise.

Harold accepted Gidget's apology and told the class if it hadn't been for the friendship, support, and trust that Franny had given him over those terrible months, he might have run away from home, or worse.

The whole class told Harold how sorry they were for their foolishness and cheered that Harold was going to be okay now. It took a long time for Harold to work through the hurt he had suffered from the gossip and rejection. He and the class had much happier days ahead than had been experienced the year before. The lessons the kids learned that year about gossip's harm would travel with them for a lifetime. It sure changed Gidget. When anyone would say to her, "Have you heard about so-and-so," she'd quickly reply, "No, and I don't want to either." "Hapless" went on to become one of the most trusted kids in Nit Picky. Years later he became a bank executive in Chicago. Sad, isn't it, how folks can so easily misjudge another?

Chapter

22 "Sneaky's" New Home

The following incident was told to our "Aged Storyteller" by Pete at a high school reunion many years after their childhood days in Nit Picky Grade School, home of the Fighting Tomcats.

"A raging snowstorm and treacherous roads kept me inside with not much more to do than remember how it used to be. Caught up in visions of former days, I sipped my hot tea as I watched the glittering flakes pile deeper on the windowsill. The Monopoly game that my wife and I had started the night before still covered one end of the kitchen table. It was that game that caused me to recall a memory of Nit Picky Grade School and a classmate, Greg Snedicur, known by most as 'Sneaky'."

Greg had been a constant agitation to Pete and the gang during their growing up days in Nit Picky. Greg was a smart kid who seemed to find schoolwork rather easy. He knew that he was a favorite to teachers due to his good grades, suave talking and handsome appearance. There was a good reason for his name "Sneaky", however; and the unfinished Monopoly game flooded Pete's mind with details of those bygone times.

In the days of the Nit Picky gang, television wasn't so available, and computer games, home computers, and the like hadn't been dreamed up yet. The kids would gather at one another's home and play games after school and on weekends. Sometimes it was physical type games, but in the winter especially, they played board games, like Scrabble, Sorry, Life, and Monopoly. "Sneaky" was a smart kid in his own right and won a lot of the time due to that fact. However, there were those times when....

Pete watched the wind lift the snow to the shed's rooftop as he recalled the day Greg slipped up. Pete, along with Milly, Franny, Phil, and Greg were playing a slow but grueling game of Monopoly. The game had been going on for some time and the play money was tight for everyone except "Sneaky", who never seemed short of funds.

"Sneaky" called the group's attention to something hanging on the wall and naturally the entire group looked that way. However, Pete was quick to lose interest in looking and returned his focus to the game board. Just as he did, he caught Greg with his hand in the bank money. Greg had always insisted on being the banker and now they knew why. "Sneaky's" face reddened as he said, "OOPS, I've been caught."

The others were fast to turn their focus from the wall to Greg. The game ended abruptly that day; the Nit Picky gang was very upset with "Sneaky's" cheating. He finally owned up to the fact that he had being doing that kind of thing for as long as he could recall.

Pete continued to remember "Sneaky" and the other kids as the January snow grew deeper on his driveway. He recalled another time when the kids of the Fighting Tomcats took a field trip to the St. Louis Zoo. Excitement had loomed at Nit Picky as the day of the field trip approached. The day finally arrived when the big yellow bus with its school logo on the sides and an emblem of the Fighting Tomcats on the back pulled up in front of the Nit Picky Grade School. Mr. "Fast Cat" drove the bus that hauled the kids and their teachers from Nit Picky to St. Louis. Pete remembered that they had left in the early hours of the morning so they could have a full day at the zoo. When they arrived, they were all lined up and given orders for this and that as they departed the bus.

By the time they reached the front of the zoo, many children and adults were lined up from other schools to go in the main gate. In those days one had to pay a quarter to get in and the zoo kept a count at the gate of the number of visitors entering. "Sneaky" was not only noted for his cheating at Monopoly, but he was quick to cheat in other ways, too. When Mr. Fulcrum, their chaperone, was distracted, "Sneaky" saw a chance to cut in line ahead of Pete. As Snedicur charged ahead of Pete, he pushed him back onto Susy's left big toe; she was wearing sandals. Naturally she let out a screeching "yee-ooooooweee" which made Mr. Fulcrum turn around so quickly that he got a bit dizzy and tripped over the fireplug in front of him. He tore his new slacks and, well you guessed it, Pete got a good verbal thrashing for causing such a ruckus. "Sneaky" unzipped his blue jacket as he smiled his Elvis Presley smile.

Now if that wasn't bad enough, as Greg entered the zoo gate just one step ahead of Pete, all creation seemed to break loose. Bells rang, sirens blared, and trumpets blew, well maybe not trumpets, but after all, Pete was remembering this through a child's eyes of many years past. He recalled that a tall important-looking man came running out of a nearby building shouting, "Stop that kid in the blue jacket!"

It happened that good old "Sneaky" had just become the first hundred-thousandth visitor to the zoo. Imagine that, and just ahead of Pete. "Sneaky" received a special zoo shirt; he made the front pages of *The St. Louis Herald*, and *The Nit Picky Weekly Tribunal*. He was even featured on the Channel Twelve news. He had his picture taken with the zoo president and Zamba the Elephant. The picture made their school yearbook.

Pete chuckled as he remembered his childhood days, but

he knew it wasn't funny at the time. Franny, along with some of the other kids had seen what had happened to him. He had turned to Franny and expressed his anger at Greg's jumping line and his constant cheating. It wouldn't have been so bad if "Sneaky" had apologized to Pete and the gang, but no, he went around boasting at his great fortune and moment of fame. Many of the teachers gloated over him for the recognition he'd brought to Nit Picky.

Pete remembered Franny sitting by him on the return trip trying to cheer him up and encourage him not to be so angry. She read Romans 12:3 to him from her small New Testament that she always carried with her. "For by the grace given me I say to every one of you: Do not think of yourself more highly than you ought, but rather think of yourself with sober judgment, in accordance with the measure of faith God has given you." Franny told Pete and the gang that "Sneaky" seemed to think of himself more highly than others and that unless that changed, it would eventually lead to serious trouble. She reasoned that his attitude led him to cheat and cut in line and things like that. She reminded Pete that the Bible was clear when it said: "Thou shalt not steal." (Exodus 20:15) Pete could never get back what Greg had taken from him that day, but as he looked back, it wasn't so important anyway. Pete was thankful that Franny had stopped him that day from returning evil for evil.

One day, some years after high school graduation, Pete read with sadness that "Sneaky" had gotten a new home. It was one with many rooms and steel bars for doors and windows. "Sneaky" had gone to prison before he was thirty. As reported in the papers and local TV news, he had been caught stealing from his boss, The Wicksburg National Bank.

When Pete sat down with his wife that wintry eve to continue their Monopoly game, he felt a sense of gratitude to the Lord. For Christ had taught him through a friend named Franny to understand that stealing from a bank, even when it was only play money, was wrong. He was thankful, too, for her encouragement not to get even with Greg, for it would have been just as wrong. Eventually, "Sneaky" straightened out his life with the help of the Lord and a prison chaplain, but so much precious time had been lost.

Chapter

23   **Unbelievable**

Rev. Watchman and his wife were awakened one Sunday at 4:30 a.m. by the R-I-N-G-I-N-G of their telephone. Startled from sleep, the preacher fumbled for the phone in the darkness. It took a moment before he realized he was saying "Hello" into the earpiece. Quickly reversing it, he repeated, "Hello, Hello".

A girl's voice said in frantic, tearful tones, "Rev. Watchman, if I don't talk to someone right away, I'm going to end my life for sure."

"What! Hold on there!" exclaimed the preacher jolting to wide awakeness. "Don't do that," he added.

"That's right, I'm so upset with my life that I can't go on, I need help, will you meet me at Joe's All-Night Diner right away?" she pleaded.

"Why yes, yes, sure, give me about fifteen minutes or so and I'll be there; I promise," the preacher said as calmly as he could while trying to slip on some clothes.

"Okay," the girl said clicking the receiver to silence.

Stubbing his little toe on the lamp table, the preacher managed to put on an unmatched pair of shoes as he rushed to get dressed and out of the house in record time. Within fifteen minutes and thirty seconds, Rev. Watchman busted into Joe's Place like an expectant father. Ignoring Joe's comments on his appearance, the Reverend's eyes surveyed the small restaurant for a distraught young girl. All he found was Rev. Bewildered who pastored the "All Right Church of the Saved" and Rev. McDifference from the "First Church of the Forgiven".

"Morning fellows," Rev. Watchman said as he scratched his head and pulled up a chair at their table. "I didn't know you fellows had coffee here at 4:50 a.m. on Sunday mornings," he said with a slight smirk on his lips.

"We don't normally," they replied in unison, "but......."

"Let me guess," interrupted Rev. Watchman, "you received a call this morning from a distressed young girl who said she was going to take her life if she didn't talk to someone."

"You, too?" they mused. "We've all been had."

The three kind-hearted ministers realized that a lie had gotten all of them out that early Sunday morning. What could they do but laugh it off as they visited and finished their coffee. They all parted, shaking hands and agreeing to get together again soon, but at a more reasonable hour during the week.

A month or so passed in the little town of Nit Picky, home of the Fighting Tomcats. Rev. and Mrs. Watchman were visiting the young widow Lucille Fibber. Her windows were open near the sofa where the Reverend and his wife were sitting. Lucille's daughter Linda and her friends were playing on the side of the house opposite the front drive and hadn't seen the Reverend pull in. Mrs. Fibber had left the room to fix some ice tea when Rev. Watchman happened to hear a voice that sounded familiar. It sounded like the girl who'd lied to him and the other preachers. She was bragging to the Nit Picky kids about her stay at Susy's house a few weekends ago. Susy lived just across the street from Joe's Place. Linda, demonstrating the voice that she had used over the phone, laughed as she told about the call to the preachers. She told them how funny it was to see all the ministers show up at the diner. Franny scolded her for pulling such a dirty trick on the town's preachers. She told her that God's word specifically tells us "not to lie or deceive one another". (Leviticus 19:11) Susy was upset, too. She hadn't known until then that Linda had gotten up and used her family's telephone to do such a mean deed.

"That's why the class calls you 'Lying' Linda," said Franny, "we can't ever believe a word you say."

"How do we even know you're not lying to us right now?" asked Milly. "You've got to stop telling all those lies!"

However, Franny and the others didn't seem to be having much effect on Linda. She just brushed them off. Then Mrs.

Fibber broke the preacher's concentration as she returned with the tea and some jellyrolls.

Rev. Watchman was saddened at what he'd heard that day, and wondered what he should do about it. After all, the widow Fibber and Linda were members of his church and it could be a sticky situation. He realized why he hadn't recognized Linda's voice that morning. She was very good at disguising it.

Two weeks after their visit to the Fibbers, Rev. and Mrs. Watchman were again awakened in the wee hours, this time on a Saturday morning.

"Rev. Watchman," began the distraught voice. "This is Linda Fibber and my house is on fire and I'm all alone."

"Oh, is that so?" replied the preacher. "How come you don't call the fire department?" he asked.

"Your number is the only one I know and I can't get to the cabinet where the phone book is kept," she panted. There was no 911 in those days.

"Linda, I know you're the one who called me a few weeks ago and I'm not falling for your lies again," exclaimed Rev. Watchman. "I'll be speaking to your mother very soon. This sort of thing has to stop. Now go back to bed and think about what you have been doing," said the distraught minister.

Later that morning Rev. Watchman was in downtown Nit Picky when he bumped into Mayor Dooalot.

"Morning, Reverend," said the mayor, "It's too bad about the Fibber's place, isn't it?"

The minister's heart seemed to skip a beat, as he asked, "What about the Fibber's place?'

"Oh," replied Mayor Dooalot, "It burnt to the ground early this morning. The girl was the only one home; her mom was working, but Linda got out okay. No one was injured, thank the Lord, but the house was a total loss, they say."

Rev. Watchman felt as if a train had hit him as he headed his car toward the Fibber's place. When he arrived, he found Linda standing alone near the tree where she loved to play. She was holding the only thing saved from the fire, her favorite teddy

bear. Her mother and some neighbors were gathered by the barn as the fire department finished their clean up work. Linda looked at the preacher through teary eyes as he came across the yard.

"I'm so sorry, Linda," cried the minister, "I should have believed you, but...." The preacher's voice trailed off.

"It's my fault," Linda cried, "not yours. It's my habit of lying that finally caught up with me. I'm sorry, too," she sobbed. "My lies to you and everyone else has cost a very high price. Rev. Watchman, can you...., well, can the Lord ever forgive me? And, what about Mother, when she finds out what I've done, will she forgive me?"

Hugging the distraught girl, Rev. Watchman said, "As far as the Lord is concerned, I know that He can and will forgive you, if you are sincere and ask him to. I can forgive you, too, but it will take time to rebuild my trust in you. Whether your mother can forgive you is something you'll have to ask her." Linda didn't notice that Mrs. Fibber had come up behind her. "This is a very serious thing you've done," said the preacher, "and it will take a long time to work through it. Telling lies is wrong."

"I know," cried Linda, "I know. Now I understand what Franny, Mom, and the others were trying to tell me and why the Lord says in His word, 'Do not lie. Do not deceive one another.'"

The Fibber place was rebuilt in time with the help of friends, neighbors and fund raising. It took much longer, however, for Linda to rebuild her trustworthiness in the lives of her mother and the others. She had learned an **expensive** lesson.

Chapter

24 Confusion in Nit Picky

Mr. Divisor was a fifty-two year old math teacher at the Nit Picky Grade School, home to the Fighting Tomcats. To the kids, he was so old that they thought for sure that he'd come over on the "Mayflower". But the kids liked Mr. Divisor even though he was strict and gave them lots of homework. They knew that he really cared for them and wanted them to succeed. He was always doing little extras for them to encourage their learning. For instance, he treated the class to ice cream on one Friday each month if they completed their homework assignments that month. He urged them to always do their best.

One day Mr. Divisor nearly scared the Nit Picky gang to death. He was working a problem on the board when he grabbed his chest in pain. He was quite pale and sweating as he slumped to the floor in front of them.

"Tommy!" he gasped, "would you run to Principal Straightshooter's office and tell him that I'm not feeling well and that I need to see the school nurse as soon as possible." Quick as electricity goes from the switch to the light, Tommy dashed to the office.

"Mr. Straightshooter," panted Tommy, "you'd better do something quick! Mr. Divisor looks and acts like the man on '*Gunsmoke*' last week. He died and the town doc said it was a heart attack." The principal, having seen the same TV program, went into a busy tizzy and called Dr. Wellman's office uptown and repeated what Tommy had said. Dr. Wellman in turn called the emergency room of Nit Picky's small clinic before he jumped into his car to rush to the school. The clinic head, Mrs. Stitches, called the local undertaker who operated the only ambulance in town. (That was long before the 911 emergency number, all the fancy ambulances, and trained emergency medical technicians.)

Being a close friend to Mr. Divisor, Bill Graveman, the undertaker, rushed to his shiny black hearse with two of his helpers, Rev. Watchman and the county coroner, Clyde Boneaker. Switching on the siren and red lights, they sped wildly toward the grade school.

In the meantime, the Nit Picky police, who had only heard the word "gun" in "Gunsmoke" on their portable radio, were also frantically racing from Joanna's Restaurant toward the school. That same "Gunsmoke" that was traveling the emergency airwaves, was fuzzy to the poor dispatcher for the Nit Picky volunteer fire department. He only caught the words "smoke" and "grade school". One can guess what happened next. Out came two big red fire trucks, the pride of Nit Picky and their town parades. One was a ladder truck with a fireman on the back steering the rear portion of the long truck. Nit picky had very few tall buildings, and the grade school was one of them. Townsfolk had made a huge fuss over the need for such a truck in their little town. But now the firemen were sure they'd prove the need for the oversized beauty.

Fire Chief Burnout was worried that their two trucks wouldn't be enough for such a "large fire" as the grade school, so he radioed Wicksburg for back up. Immediately they sent two of their largest tanker trucks and thirty of their top firemen, including a safety-net crew to catch any jumpers.

A county sheriff's deputy picked up the emergency call. His radio was so plagued with static that he only heard "jumping

110

from the roof of the Nit Picky Grade School." He immediately notified his dispatcher at the county office that there was a suicide attempt at the Nit Picky Grade School and that he and five other units were speeding toward the school.

In the meantime, Mr. Divisor had been given a drink of water and was fanned by the Nit Picky gang in his classroom. Franny asked, "Mr. Divisor, why don't you loosen your tie a bit, it looks awfully tight today. In fact," she continued, "I noticed that your shirt looks like it's too small or something."

Mr. Divisor thought for a minute as he was trying to catch his breath. "You know, I did get dressed in quite a hurry in the dark this morning," he said. "Power was off again." He took off his sports coat, and low and behold, the sleeves on his shirt were well above his wrists. "Why, I have on my son's shirt," he declared "and it's two sizes too small for me." The relieved teacher laughed with the kids as he said, "No wonder my chest feels tight and I can hardly breath." He released the tight collar and the color came to his face immediately. The pain in his chest vanished with the breeze that was blowing through the classroom windows.

But what was all the racket coming into the room on that same breeze? Sirens of all pitches could be heard from blocks away. The kids and Mr. Divisor scurried to the windows as the sirens neared the school.

"There must be a terrible accident or fire," said Frank.

All of a sudden and right in front of their school, the kids saw the most remarkable sight. They watched in awe as the ambulance, three Nit Picky police cars, Dr. Wellman's car with its blue light flashing, six county police cars, two town fire trucks including the ladder truck, two Wicksburg fire trucks, and hordes of scared parents surrounded their school. Several firemen were carrying axes, some were lugging hoses, and a trampoline-like item was being rushed to the base of the school.

Before they could hardly turn from the window, the kids and Mr. Divisor witnessed three firemen, two policemen, the doctor, the preacher, the coroner, and the undertaker all rush into their now-crowded classroom. They had Mr. Divisor's shirt removed and him stretched out on the gurney before he could make them understand that his red face was from embarrassment and that his chest pains had been from an overly tight collar. The emergency workers finally understood why the kids were laughing so hard. The whole event made the Channel Twelve News that night and was no doubt the topic of conversation at all the Nit Picky supper tables.

The next day's math class was more of a discussion group than a division lesson. The children and Mr. Divisor were amazed at how things had gotten so confused the day before. They decided that the main problem was due to poor communication. Franny said that she wished that the excitement and concern everyone had had when they felt there was a serious need at the grade school would carry over into people's concern for the unsaved, the lonely, and the hurting condition of people's spiritual hearts. Mr. Divisor commented on how tangled and misunderstood the communication had become. The children compared that to the dangers of gossip or not listening closely to others, or reacting to something in haste without checking out the facts. Milly Snodgrass chimed in that she felt the poor communication taught her that Christians needed to be especially careful how they talked and behaved around others so as to not confuse them about the love and salvation of the Lord. Mr. Divisor said that he learned to watch his shirt labels more closely, not get in such a hurry, and always dress in the light, even if he had to use candles.

Franny said, "The Bible teaches us 'above all else, guard your heart, for it is the wellspring of life.'" (Proverbs 4:23) She went on to say, "We should all read God's word more carefully for it's one way God communicates his instructions to us. If we don't read God's word and pray and listen to him," she said, "we might get his messages all confused. We might do something that will cause others as well as ourselves serious pain like the tight collar caused Mr. Divisor."

Tommy, who had recently accepted Christ as his Savior made perhaps the best observation. He said, "Yesterday taught me that people often get so caught up in solving their own problems that they miss the simple solution right before their eyes, their need for Jesus. He is the only one who can loosen the devil's strangle hold around our necks and help us to breathe the breath of eternal life."

For the kid's help, Mr. Divisor gave them ice cream, the kind that came in paper cups with pull-tab lids and wooden spoons. Then the bell rang and class was over for another day.

Chapter

25   "Devil Lady"

Not too far from the Nit Picky Grade School stood a decaying house that was nearly concealed by its unkempt yard. The short rock wall that had once neatly surrounded the house was nothing more than piles of stone. Tangled vines and briars covered most of it. One rusted hinge separated its forlorn iron gate from loss to the weeds. In the wintertime one could see the deteriorating car, deserted appliances, and assorted junk, which had been hidden by the summer's foliage. The steep roof of the aged house was missing more than a few shingles. Its attic window had cardboard taped over the broken glass. The disturbing house was frightening, especially on a moonlit night. That house on the corner of Pine and Wolf streets was known by the town's folk as the spook house of Nit Picky.

Occasionally, the Nit Picky gang would see a pale, white-haired, bony-figured woman peek through the torn curtains of the upstairs windows. The kids of Nit Picky, home of the Fighting Tomcats, called her the "Devil Lady". They had all kinds of scary stories about the mysterious woman, but no one really knew much about her. Few of the children ever saw her away from her house and when they did they'd walk on the opposite side of the street. Sometimes the kids would throw rocks at her house and yell, "'Devil Lady', 'Devil Lady'", then run like scared jackrabbits. Her voice would crack, as she yelled at the fleeing kids. "Mean" Mike had managed to break a window.

One day the Nit Picky gang noticed a fresh pile of junk at the back edge of the "Devil Lady's" place. "Nosy" Nelly and "Mean" Mike led the gang's search of the intriguing discovery. Susy kept watch for the unwanted appearance of its owner. It didn't take long for them to spot the ancient trunk. Breaking it open, their eyes widened as they found faded pictures, dried-flowers, yellowed-papers and stacks of letters bound by string. Mike let out a yelp when he opened a small box at the bottom of the trunk. It contained a tarnished compass and a tattered map. It had an "X" that marked the spot, like all mysterious old maps should. The kids almost ripped it apart in their excited attempt to be the first to study it.

Nelly said, "There's no doubt, it's a treasure map all right. From the trees listed and street location, it's a map of the 'Devil Lady's' yard."

Even Franny found the "kid" in her getting excited over the whole idea of a buried treasure. Although the gang knew it was wrong and quite dangerous, they decided to do the forbidden. They'd meet Friday night and cross behind the rock wall into the "Devil Lady's" wilderness. Franny was hesitant at first, yet her curiosity was peaked by the mysterious "X".

"After all," the kids reasoned, "the lady threw the map away and we can't hurt her messy yard." It was decided they'd have a camp-out in "Clutts" Clinkmyer's yard and quietly slip away after his parents were asleep.

Friday night, with a shovel, a flashlight, some rope, and the map, the gang made their way through the jungle of tangled brush and junk. They hacked at the weeds until they reached the large oak tree shown in the center of the map. It was under that tree that two steps north and three steps east would end at the coveted "X". "Fearless" Frank's hand was fast in covering Milly's mouth when a snake slithered past gripping its captured prey, a mouse. Nick snagged his leg on the edge of a discarded garden plow and drew a small trace of blood. "Greedy" Gerty was awarded a face full of cobwebs for her efforts to out step the others. Gidget sneezed and in unison the gang said, "Shuuuuu!" Their eyes enlarged to saucer-size as an owl asked, "Who, who?"

Finally, they reached the monstrous oak and quickly stepped off the anticipated directions. It led them to a large rock. The treasure had to be under it, they reasoned. Pushing with all their strength, the stubborn boulder wouldn't budge. Lonnie suggested that they toss their rope over the low branch of the tree and tie it around the rock. He said that with all of them pulling together they could pry the rock loose, then swing it off to the side. What they didn't see in the darkness, however, was that the lower limb was not only large, it was dead.

With a thunderous crash the heavy limb gave way under the kids' weight. Never had a group of children moved faster than did the Nit Picky gang. But "Mean" Mike wasn't fast enough. He now lay on the damp ground with his leg pinned beneath the entrapping limb. The children gasped in fear when a light came on in the "Devil Lady's" house and they heard her shaky voice call out, "W-h-o's o-u-t t-h-e-r-e?"

Following a slim ray of light that waved back and forth, a shadowy figure was closing in on them. The limb wouldn't surrender to their frightened efforts. Suddenly, she stood there, looking every bit as scary as the kids had ever imagined. A slight shriek left her lips as she saw Mike beneath that limb and his friends helpless to rescue him. Instead of chasing them with a broomstick, as they expected, the woman knelt down by Mike, patted his trembling arm and talked to him like a loving mother. The gang stood in frozen disbelief.

"Hurry," she said to Franny. "Go to the house, use the phone in the kitchen and call the police, their number is on the phone. Tell them we need an ambulance and manpower." Then she asked the kids for a jacket to put under Mike's head and another to cover his shivering body. She caressed his forehead and spoke comforting words to the sobbing boy. She directed Susy to scurry to the kitchen and get Mike some water and a towel to wipe the dirt from his face. For several moments the children acted as if they were petrified, their mouths gaped open in shock at the kindness of their "Devil Lady."

Flashing red lights announced that help had arrived for Mike and his nightmarish situation. His leg was broken, but other than that he was not seriously injured. To say the kids were in trouble with their parents would be an understatement. But they were glad that their children were safe and that Mike wasn't critical. The parents and kids were especially grateful to the "Devil Lady" who they learned was Mrs. Grace Moorely.

Several days later, with Mike on crutches, the gang went over to visit Mrs. Moorely to apologize for their bad behavior and trespassing on her property. She offered them homemade cookies and milk as they explained what they had been doing in her yard. They were amazed at her aged frame as she started shaking with laughter.

"That old map," she said, "belonged to my husband and his Boy Scout troop. He had used it in his compass training exercises years ago."

"Then there never was a treasure?" asked Franny.

117

"Never," the lady snickered in an endearing way. Her eyes actually sparkled as she enjoyed the kids' company. The gang perhaps learned one of the greatest lessons of their young lives. They had judged that dear lady by outer conditions and appearances, without even knowing her. It turned out that Grace's husband was killed in an accident several years earlier; she never remarried. They hadn't had any children and her parents died some thirty years ago. Grace was left alone and with little money. Over the years, things had gone downhill for her, especially the house.

The children realized that they had made a new friend, a white-haired lady who needed their help. Phil took the lead with Franny in organizing a plan to help Mrs. Moorely get her place fixed up. The community followed the children's lead and within months, the house that had looked haunted now looked like a picture in *Better Homes and Gardens.*

And the large rock, where the gang had met Grace? Well, Mrs. Grace let them paint a blue "X" right on top of it. Mike painted this gesture, stating that truly they had found a real treasure in that spot, friendship with an "Angel Lady." The kids made painting the rock into a "big" ceremony. They even made peanut-butter sandwiches and lemonade for the occasion. As part of the event, Franny read the following scripture from 1 Samuel 16:7 "But the LORD said to Samuel, 'Do not consider his appearance or his height, for I have rejected him. The LORD does not look at the things man looks at. Man looks at the outward appearance, but the LORD looks at the heart.'"

Franny said, "God wants us to look beyond skin color, language, age, and gender. He wants us to love one another and to help each other. After all, that kind of love is truly the very best of treasures."

Mrs. Moorely's home and yard became one of the kids' favorite places in all of Nit Picky.

Chapter

26   Nit Picky's Big Party

One day and counting! The classroom calendar was full of multicolored "X's" hurriedly scratched each day by whomever thought of it first. Milly Snodgrass was quick to mark a bright red "X" right through Friday, May 28th, as she and her classmates scrambled into Mr. Dustberger's history class. The next night was to be the end-of-the-school-year party at Nit Picky Grade School, home of the Fighting Tomcats. This was no small celebration; it was the party of parties. Over the years this annual event had grown into a community-wide event.

There were games, prizes, a sock hop in the gym, and food to everyone's liking. Small towns like Nit Picky looked for reasons to celebrate, and this party had become one.   To top off the evening's events, there was a burger-eating contest sponsored by the "What-A-Burger" for any eighth grade boy crazy enough to try it. They had to have a permission slip from home, of course, just in case they made themselves sick.

Ten boys had taken the challenge to beat "Clutts" Clinkmyer's boast that he was hamburger king of Nit Picky. It was true that "Clutts" never did take "THE HILL" with his bike, however, without a doubt, he was the "man" to be reckoned with when it came to eating hamburgers of any size or quantity.

One character who had grown up in Nit Picky, all eight grades, was Billy; better known by the other kids as "Bashful" Billy. He was such a bashful kid that even talking to a girl turned him strawberry red. The only girl he had ever kissed was when they were in the first grade and that was only due to a "double-dog-dare" by his buddies. The kids remembered that Billy's cheeks remained red for an entire week after that. His mother thought he was ill.

But Billy was sweet on a blonde-haired girl in the eighth grade by the name of Kelly Stearnfellow. The boys all called her "Cutesy". She always wore her hair in pigtails and was perhaps the cutest girl in all of Nit Picky. That was a common opinion, too, and not just that of Billy's. Kelly knew about the nickname, but never let it puff up her pride; that was part of her charm.

Many a boy wanted to take "Cutesy" Kelly to the big party, but wouldn't you know it? Billy, of all fellows, caught a brave moment and had been the first to ask her. It had taken all the courage that young fellow could muster in his life, but he, "Bashful" Billy, actually asked her to the big party. and wonder of wonders she had said yes.

There was a catch, however. Because she was so young, Kelly's dad wouldn't let her go with any boy unless they were with another couple. Billy wasn't worried about that little clause in the agreement; he had several friends that could help him out.

But Friday the 28th had arrived, and Billy was still without the second couple to go with them to the party. He was beginning to sweat buckets knowing that he would have to face "Cutesy's" dad alone if no other couple was found. Billy really couldn't concentrate on Mr. Dustberger's lesson that day on Lincoln's farewell address to Spokane, Washington, or wherever it was that he was leaving (actually it was Springfield, Illinois).

Saturday came and Billy was on the phone and then door to door. He had gone from his closest buddies to strangers on the street, but no one was available to go with him and Kelly. "Bashful" Billy was getting desperate! He was to go to Kelly's house at four o'clock sharp to walk her to the big party.

High noon came and went; Billy had heard so many excuses of why this one and that one couldn't go with him. He was beginning to wonder if some space ship had landed and hoodwinked all his friends and turned them against him. Two o'clock came and he had to get ready to face Mr. Stearnfellow, Kelly's dad. What would he say or do? Billy's knees were shaking so badly that they air-dried after his bath before he could take a towel to them.

Four o'clock came and "Bashful" Billy stood at Kelly's front door. With great effort, he knocked. There she stood, all dressed up and ready to go. Kelly had to be the prettiest girl in town. But right behind Kelly towered her father, all six-foot four, two hundred and eighty pounds of him.

"Mr. Stearnfellow," began Billy in his shakiest voice ever, "I have run into a small problem. I couldn't get another couple to go with us no matter how hard I tried." Continuing he added, "But, I really do want to take your daughter to the party." By now Billy was leaning against a porch post for support.

"Well," began Kelly's father in his deep bass voice that could shake one's flesh at twenty paces. "This is quite unusual to say the least, and you know the rules, don't you?"

121

"Y-e-s, s-i-r," squeaked Billy.

"However," Mr. Stearnfellow began again, "since I have known you and your family for many years, and because of your good reputation, I'm going to remove the rule for this one time just for you. But just for tonight! Understand?"

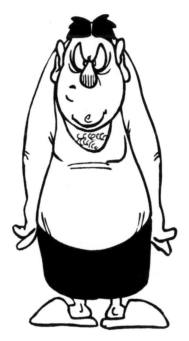

"Yes, Sir!" Billy said, smiling from ear to ear and feeling like he should salute the man.

"Bashful" Billy and Kelly had the best time ever at the party. Strangest thing, though, all those buddies who had excuses about not going, were there with their girls, except for "Tricky" Tom Hullagan. Tom was there, but without a partner.

"That's strange," mused Billy, "I thought Tom was friends with Susy and would have asked her to the party."

Come to find out, old "Tricky" Tom was also sweet on "Cutesy" and had wanted to take her to the party himself. Billy learned later that his and Tom's buddies owed Tom a bunch of favors, and he had demanded their pay back. Unknown to Billy,

Tom had pressured all the fellows in class to say no to "Bashful's" request to double date with him and Kelly.

"What a dirty, low-down jealous trick to play!" Billy exclaimed. He was deeply hurt and angered to think that his friends would agree to such a scheme, especially after all their years as classmates.

Franny learned of the mischief and was very disappointed in the fellows. She talked to Billy and helped him see how the trick had backfired and how only he had been able to escort Kelly to the party by himself. Franny reminded Billy that Jesus would respond to such ugliness by turning the other cheek. She warned him of the danger of holding onto anger and malice. She shared with him the following Bible verse: "Get rid of all bitterness, rage and anger, brawling and slander, along with every form of malice. Be kind and compassionate to one another, forgiving each other, just as in Christ God forgave you." (Ephesians 4:31-32)

"Bashful" Billy never did forget that experience, but he chose, in Christ, to forgive and be kind even to "Tricky" Tom. Billy learned that the way you treat others is very important to Jesus. He realized that how you react to what others do to you is more important in your life than what they did. He listened to Franny and sought Christ's help in overcoming his anger and bitterness. Besides, Franny was right, he'd had the best time.

In the years to come, Billy lost his shyness. He married that little blonde-haired girl named Kelly. Billy became a Christian counselor and witnessed many times the tragic results of angry hearts and bitter-unforgiving spirits.

Chapter

27   The Cliff

The "Aged Storyteller" of these *Adventures in Nit Picky* received the following account in a letter from Dan Wallis, a former classmate. It took place forty years or so after they had graduated from the eighth grade of the Nit Picky Grade School, home of the Fighting Tomcats.

After a visit to Nit Picky to pay respects to an old friend, Dan found himself taking a back road until he and his wife reached highway 287.   He headed the car northward.   The memories stirred by that stretch of two-lane road brought tears to his tired eyes. His wife started to speak, but paused; she knew he was remembering. Dan wondered if it was still there, that rocky ridge, that cliff, which had once stood like a mountain to his childhood vision.

His question was soon answered as he rounded the sharp bend in the road. A half-mile or so in the distance stood the jagged cliff as it had in years past, only it was much shorter than he remembered. Its surface reflected the afternoon sun.

Clicking on the left turn signal, Dan Wallis slowed to make a turn onto the graveled area by the cliff's base. He parked his Lincoln Continental near the weathered hill and for a few moments he and his wife stared through the open sunroof at the high pinnacle of rock. Then Dan opened the car door and slowly climbed out. Standing next to the car for support, he examined that weather-beaten slope. Scraggly, twisted cedar trees clung to the cliff's edge, framing it like a picture. A few more of their kind had managed to spring from the sloped surface of the staunch spectacle.

Wallis remembered his childhood days in Nit Picky with Franny, "Clutts", Milly, Phil, Susy, and the rest of gang. Most of them he'd not seen since their high school graduation. Dan recalled his nickname in those days, it was "Someday"; yes, the kids had called him "Someday" Danny. He had earned the nickname legitimately as a kid. The nickname described him accurately, and he had lived to regret it. In fact, the old cliff was one good reason for his disappointing, yet descriptive, nickname.

The rocky cliff was on the road that had led to his grandmother's house. Dan's folks usually took him there a couple of times a month to visit his grandmother and blind great-grandmother. Every time his family would drive by that cliff, "Someday" Danny would dream how someday he would climb it and explore its rocks and trees and caves. He knew that he'd find lizards, snakes, arrowheads, and "lucky" rocks.

But the years sped quickly by as page after page of Danny's life tore away. One might guess, "Someday" Danny never did find the time to climb that cliff and explore its hidden mysteries. There were always places to go, work to do, money to be made, and a life to be lived. The cliff waited, but Danny never came. Now as Dan, with cane in hand, peered at that ragged cliff through bifocaled eyes, he realized that finally he had the time. Sad, however, was the truth that he no longer had the strength to ascend that mystical rock.

He had been "Someday" Danny in so many things as a youth. His friends had learned not to take too much stock in what he said or planned. They knew it would be some day in an imaginary future before he would ever get around to doing it. Oh, Dan had lots of good intentions in his day for helping others and doing good deeds and showing kindness, but the love of money and the drive for more always shoved everything else into

125

his some-day file.

Now, like a bronzed statue, "Someday" Danny stood, rich, successful, but very sorry over his lost some-days. The cliff seemed to laugh at him as the wind whistled through its twisted trees and rocks.

"Franny had been right, you know," wrote Dan. "She told me and demonstrated by her own actions how to put God first in ones' life. She encouraged me to enjoy the simple things, to climb the cliffs, to look up to the sky on a starry night, and to smell the rain on a summer's day. Franny had asked me to take time to believe in and serve Jesus. She challenged me to make the effort to help and enjoy others, but I didn't listen. In fact, I laughed at her. A verse of scripture that she always preached to me is still in my head. 'Remember your Creator in the days of your youth, before the days of trouble come and the years approach when you will say, I find no pleasure in them.' (Ecclesiastes 12:1) But I spent my youthful life on selfish, get-rich schemes, which left everything else for some other time."

Dan's letter concluded, "The good news is that I have finally found my 'some day' in the Lord. Franny's witness and the Lord's call never totally left me and I recently accepted the love of Christ into my old heart. The bad news is that I have so few 'some days' left to put that love to good use for others."

Oh, that Franny could have read Dan's letter. She had made the best of her "somedays", taking each day as a blessing from the Lord. The "somedays" that she had taken to share with Danny Wallis had not been wasted after all. They never are when one does what the Lord wants.

The "Aged Storyteller" preserved Dan's letter and used it many times to encourage others not to wait for "some day", but to follow the Lord each new day. Dan's widow wrote the next letter from the Wallis family to the "Storyteller". Life is short.

Chapter

28　Letter from Texas

A month had passed and none of the Nit Picky gang had heard a word from Bobby. He had moved to Cityville, a suburb of Houston, Texas, late that summer. Bobby's dad had been transferred to his company's main office before school had ended last spring. Bobby's family had stayed behind in order for him to finish school and for his dad to have time to find a suitable place for them to live.

Like most of the Nit Picky kids, Bobby had a nickname; the gang called him "Bigot" Bobby. He and his Dad were noted for being critical and outspoken about folks of different nationalities. They especially disliked large cities that were filled with people who spoke foreign languages. That's one reason Bobby's dad had moved them to Nit Picky in the first place. The kids were all wondering how such a location change would work with their former classmate. Bobby was a likable fellow, but he was really hung up on the issue of different nationalities.

When the kids of Nit Picky Grade School, home of the Fighting Tomcats, had asked Bobby about his dislike for foreigners, he told them about being ripped off at a carnival by a fellow who couldn't speak but a few words in English.

"You just can't trust any of them people from other countries," he'd say to all that'd listen. Funny, isn't it, how one incident in life and the influence of others can shade one's feelings toward a whole group of folks? But that's how it was with Bobby. He was just downright rude to anyone who had an accent other than his own. The kids couldn't imagine how he would survive Cityville. Franny had done her best, along with their pastor, Rev. Watchman, to help Bobby overcome his bigotry. Franny had prayed that God would do something to help Bobby see his non-Christ-like attitude. The Nit Picky gang waited for some word concerning Bobby and his family.

On the tenth day of school, Mrs. Playwright announced that she had a surprise for the class during their homeroom time. The kids loved surprises; Mike hoped it was cake and ice cream. Susy hoped it was a one-way trip for the boys to another planet. Homeroom time came and Mrs. Playwright held up a letter postmarked Cityville, Texas. The excited kids were eager to learn about Bobby as she began reading his letter:

Dear Mrs. Playwright and Nit Picky gang,

The trip to Cityville was one I'll never forget. We drove two whole days, and I only got carsick four times. Mom said that the car would smell better in a week or two. The motel we stayed in was shabby; the pool was cracked and we couldn't swim. Our cat, Furry, chased a mouse in our room all night. Dad threw his shoe at her but broke a mirror instead. I think he was mad that he had to pay for it. He mumbled under his breath.

The trailer we pulled worked okay, except for the flat tire we had just as we got to Cityville. It wouldn't have been so bad, but it was at a time that Dad called rush hour. All I know was that there were billions of cars on the road around us all honking their Texas horns to greet us. I thought that was nice of them, but Dad turned red and mumbled under his breath again. Mom shushed him; she did that a lot. Several of the folks that passed us shouted and shook their fists at us. Mom said it was the way Texan's waved at new folks, but that seemed strange to me.

After fixing the tire, we started out again, only to find that we had missed our turn and were lost. Dad said we weren't lost, but only trying a new way. Mom wanted him to stop and ask directions, but Dad started mumbling again. I needed to use the bathroom really bad, and Dad didn't want to stop for that, either.

I think he was still upset over my getting sick on the back seat. Finally he stopped, but the bathroom was out of order. Dad turned cherry red. Mom said it was probably because of the 105-degree heat here in Texas.

The filling station guy let me use the girl's restroom, yuck! I tried not to touch anything. I shouldn't tell you fellows about that; I just hope you never have to do that. I'm still embarrassed about it.

Once we finally reached our new home, things really got interesting. When Dad went to lift the trailer door, it was jammed and wouldn't rise over 12 inches or so. Dad yanked off his ball cap, threw it down and stomped on it until the St. Louis Cardinal's emblem only read "St." Mom said that it was a sign from God. In the excitement, I forgot to shut the car door and Furry, our cat, shot out to the nearby park and went up a tree.

She's okay though; the firemen smiled as they handed her back to us. The fire chief told Dad there would be a $50 fee for making the call since Furry didn't have Texas tags. Dad turned red and grumbled again. He did that a lot.

Dad finally got the trailer door unjammed by racing the car forward and then slamming on the brakes. The apartment folks told him that the cost of cleaning up the tire marks he'd made would be added to our next month's rent. And Mom told Dad that she could clean up the coffee spill on the seat. Dad's face was glowing red again as he mumbled even more.

Since we didn't know anyone in Texas, Mom, Dad, and I had to move all our belongings into the apartment by ourselves.

Even though we had sold most of our furniture, we still had a lot of stuff. Did I mention that dad had rented us an apartment on the fourth floor? The place doesn't even have elevators! When I kept telling Dad that there were 200 steps up to our apartment, Mom shushed me and said count again. Dad was turning crimson and grumbling even more, so I shut up. We only unloaded a small part of our stuff the first night, because we'd lost so much time with Furry's rescue and the trailer door.

We had army cots to sleep on for the first night. Dad had gotten them cheap at the army surplus store. His cot collapsed sometime after midnight. By the way he danced around after hitting the floor, I guessed that he was okay. Mom just told me to keep quiet. She did that a lot.

The next morning the moving went well until Mom and I dropped an oak bookcase that Dad had built in high school. We were lucky; it only fell three flights of stairs. Neighbors frowned at us through their windows. Dad grinned through his pearly-white teeth and red face. He said that it was okay, someone could probably use the firewood. Dad is so thoughtful like that.

We're all moved in now and things are better. If I sound a little different in my letter, it's because of what God did near the end of this move. We had carried almost everything up those four flights of stairs, (actually there were only 48 steps in all,) when we came to the last two pieces of furniture. I couldn't budge them and neither could Mom. Dad grunted and struggled, but it was no use, we just couldn't move them, we were so tired and hot. Dad was bright red and mumbling again.

Mom just smiled and kept repeating, "Now, now, God will work it all out."

I used to hate it when she'd say that, but not anymore. For out of no where, appeared two giant, olive-colored men with dark beards, long hair, and nose rings. They had been moving a couch into a first floor apartment. Lucky stiffs, I thought. They were talking to each other, but we couldn't understand a word they said. My first foreigners, I mumbled and so did Dad. Mom shushed us both; I hate when she does that!

But would you believe it, those two foreigners came over

and asked us, in broken English of course, if we could use their help. We stopped mumbling and with a tired nod, said yes. As quick as you can imagine, those two giants had the rest of our heavy stuff up those stairs and into our new home. Dad insisted that they take two dollars for their help; they didn't want to, but Dad stuck it in the older man's shirt pocket. He thanked us. They really were nice and sincere in wanting to help us. Boy did they ever help us. I knew Dad was happy, because two dollars would have bought us a whole meal at a "What-A-Burger" in Texas. Dad wasn't red or mumbling any longer.

Franny, I just wanted you and Rev. Watchman to know that I have finally understood the verse of scripture you both preached to me. You know the one in Galatians 3:28 that says: "There is neither Jew nor Greek, slave nor free, male nor female, for you are all one in Christ Jesus." One shouldn't judge anyone by his or her speech, color, or appearance, it's what's on the inside that really matters after all.

I miss you all very much, but I am making some new friends, and some of them even speak English! Tee Hee!

Your friend, Bobby

P.S. The kids down here have given me a new nickname: "Bigheart". They call me "Bigheart" Bobby.

Chapter

29   A Life that was Missed

Many years ago in the little town of Nit Picky, home of the Fighting Tomcats, there lived a young girl by the name of Missy Alright, but, most of the kids called her "Missit". Even her parents frequently used "Missit" instead of her real name because of her unusual birth. On their way to the hospital in Wicksburg, Mr. Alright had missed a turn and Missy was born in a police car that her dad had flagged down.

Missy's classmates marveled at how well her name reflected her personality and defined her character so accurately.

"Missit" Alright was exceptional at missing things. She wasn't absentminded or anything like that. "Missit" had another problem that caused her to miss everything. For example, there was the time of the Nit Picky Grade School Christmas trip to St. Louis, Missouri.

The holidays were fast approaching, and the seventh and eighth grade classes were a-buzz over their upcoming field trip. The outing involved catching a train at Wicksburg to St. Louis to see the Christmas displays in the store windows. Back in those days, the St. Louis merchants elaborately decorated their windows with animated characters and Christmas decor that drew crowds from miles around. Not only would the Nit Picky gang see the many lights, they also would have the opportunity to talk to a department store Santa. Each child would be given a small present and some candy. The children were to dine in a fancy restaurant, and ice cream was to be served on the train ride home. The kids wouldn't return to Nit Picky until 1:30 a.m. The children talked of little else but the trip and how late they would get to stay out. Some of the kids hadn't been able take the train trip to Chicago, so this would be their first train ride. The St. Louis trip was like a Christmas present for many of the children.

When the exciting day arrived, their yellow school bus waited at the curb to take them from Nit Picky to the Wicksburg station. "Missit" took her seat by the window. "Fast Cat" the driver would be dropping them off and picking them up from the train station. The seat next to "Missit" was the last to be filled, few classmates ever wanted to sit by her for reasons yet to be described. It befell Linda Fibber's fate to sit beside Missy. Right away she came to life by telling Linda how she disliked the bus driver. It seemed that "Missit" and Mr. "Fast Cat" had argued over her bad behavior on the bus some few months earlier. "Missit" just wouldn't forget it! She fussed about their driver all the way to the train station. Linda wondered how one individual could find so much bad to say about another person.

Caught up in her unforgiving spirit, "Missit" missed the deer that were grazing in a field just outside of Nit Picky. She missed the red fox drinking from the Nit Picky creek. Missed were the rabbits that raced the bus to its next turn. Missy never

saw the geese that flew over the bus in perfect V-formation. So engrossed in her tale of woe, Missy even failed to enjoy the huge snowflakes that stuck to the bus windows.

When they boarded the train, Missy spotted Phil with no seat partner and rushed to sit by him. She made no secret of her fondness for him. Phil was less than thrilled, but, what was he to do? Missy had him trapped between the aisle and the window. Phil politely asked her if she had seen the beautiful deer.

"There were deer? I just love deer. I missed them?" Missy sighed and quickly changed subjects as she asked, "Phil, can I sit by the window?"

"Well, I guess," Phil muttered as they struggled to squeeze past each other between the seats.

"Phil, this seat is dirty!" she exclaimed as she stared at where he had been sitting. "Did you know how dirty this seat was? You tricked me into trading with you, didn't you? I want my seat back! I won't sit in such a dirty one," whined Miss "Missit." The seat was simply stained from age and use. It wouldn't have soiled one's clothing. In fact, it wasn't much different than the rest of the seats on the old train car.

Phil reluctantly traded seats with her for a second time, suffering through the squeezing process once again. By the time she was all settled, the train had passed through Nit Picky itself. The other children had cheered at seeing their own town from the train's perspective. Some of their parents, including Missy's, had been on the old station platform waving as they went past. But, Missy missed it, and so did Phil!

"Phil," Missy continued, "don't you think the train is a bit cold and the seats are too hard? And what is all that racket it makes, clickity clack, clickity clack; it's driving me crazy. I wish I hadn't come on this smelly old train," nagged Missy, as she continued to vibrate Phil's aching eardrums.

Phil mumbled gruffly under his breath, "I wish you hadn't either, Missy dear!"

"What did you say, Phil Fooseberry?" Missy asked.

Quick thinking, Phil replied, "I wish you hadn't missed the deer either. Whew, that was close," he thought.

A snack cart was wheeled down the aisle. The friendly porter in his sharp black outfit and red cap came to Phil and "Missit's" row. "What will you have, young lady?" he asked with a smile.

"What do you have, mister?" Missy blurted back.

Patiently, the porter went through a long list of goodies that anyone could have easily seen on his cart.

Missy harshly complained, "There's nothing I like!"

Meanwhile, Phil chose a Babe Ruth candy bar, some

136

chips and an RC Cola. The cart moved on. Missy had missed the snack. She spent the rest of the trip complaining about the poor selection of snacks offered and the fact that she hadn't received any. Missy whined at how dirty the floor was, and how worn the armrest was, and how..... Phil had no chance to speak, not that he wanted too, least-wise to Missy. He let his mind drift off to a far-away enchanted island in the Pacific Ocean that had lots of buried treasure, pirates, sandy beaches, and NO MISSY! Phil's daydreaming helped him shut out her constant complaints.

The sun's light was going out as they arrived in St. Louis. There was just enough time to make it to the restaurant and eat before their tour of the stores. Phil managed to escape Missy, but she continued her complaining to "Clutts", Milly, and Franny. She covered topics like the noisy streets, the cold winds, the fishy river smell, the..... Missy missed the beautifully decorated entrance to the fancy eatery. Missed was her choice of drinks being served at the restaurant; she received only a glass of water. What about the toy train that circled the beautifully decorated tree not far from their table? She missed it, too.

Her French fries were too cold; her burger was too hot, the ketchup wouldn't flow, and the mustard wouldn't stop. Missy failed to hear the charming Christmas carols sung by the choir of school children that had been invited to sing for them.

On the street the children were "oohing" and "aahing" at the animated figures in the huge storefronts. Santas moved, reindeer flew, nutcrackers cracked, sugarplums danced, and Christmas trees twirled. However, poor "Missit" Alright didn't see any of it. She was too absorbed in the trash that had been carelessly tossed onto the streets.

"How dare anyone be so sloppy," she exclaimed. "People ought to be arrested for that," she nagged. Stepping in to some discarded gum, she really fussed.

Missy complained about the hobo on the street corner rattling his tin cup for a donation. "I can't believe he's begging right here on the city streets and in front of us. I'm not giving him a dime of my spending money," she preached on, missing the beautiful window displays and their magical fantasy and music. She missed the children's laughter and the brightly wrapped packages of passing shoppers and the bells of the Salvation Army.

When the group arrived at the department store Santa, they smiled with joy even though they knew he was only one of the many Christmas helpers. However, Missy felt like his fake beard was too scraggily, his suit was too faded and his belly too skinny. She let it be known that she wasn't having her picture made with that Santa! And, the present he gave each of the children, a neat little Santa watch, didn't suit her either.

She complained so much to Mr. Claus that he took the watch back, gave her a candy cane and said, "Sorry kid! **Next!**" The candy cane was sour lemon. The department store Santa grinned behind his fake beard as he handed it to her. He only gave that flavor to SPECIAL CHILDREN.

The children and their chaperones had to run to catch their train. Most laughed with glee, but Missy whined that it hurt her legs and was un-lady-like. By now, one may have guessed,

Missy didn't like the choices of ice cream offered on the train ride home either. She was so busy complaining about the whole trip that she missed all the pretty Christmas lights in the little towns they passed through. She missed the full moon that peeped through the clouds. The fussy child also overlooked the snow that glistened in the moon's light.

"Missit" gave Susy an ear full about Mr. "Fast Cat", the bus driver as the old bus delivered its cargo from the Wicksburg station back to the Nit Picky Grade School at 1:45 a.m.

"Fifteen minutes late," complained Missy.

She had missed the entire Christmas trip. While the other children excitedly told their parents about their adventures and showed them their new watches, Missy sauntered off to her house just a few doors from the school.

Later, when the Nit Picky gang was together for lunch, Franny said, "Sad, isn't it, how some people go their entire lives missing the beauty of the world around them and the kindness in others? They miss the joys, the friendships, the happy moments, the good things of life? In focusing on the negative things in life, they miss all the good." Franny continued sharing her wisdom, "When one hangs onto unforgiveness over past hurts, mistakes, sins and flaws of others, they really do miss life's trip. When all that a person sees is the bad of the day, and never the good, they miss everything, even Jesus. While a person only looks inward, downward, or backward, they fail to look upward toward Christ."

Franny helped the kids discover a truth she had learned in her own life: "…if …you seek the LORD your God, you will find him if you look for him with all your heart and with all your soul." (Deuteronomy 4:29)

But "Missit" Alright was one that, as far as anyone knows, never did find Christ's good in anyone or anything. She truly missed her life's journey. Most of the Nit Picky kids lost track of Missy over the years. Some say that she ended up in a special home for the unhappy, never content and complaining about everything, especially the sudden blast of **heat** that she said she was experiencing when she died.

Chapter

30   A Valentine for Hal

Stocky built, Hal stood five foot three and a half inches. His dark-caverned eyes peered past his peaked nose and up-turned mouth. A set of ears jutted from his round head; stuck on as if an after thought.   Speckled with freckles, his fair-complexioned face was topped by short, fire-red hair that was always flat on top. He wore sunglasses and a black leather jacket winter and summer.   It was rumored that Hal bathed once every two weeks, but his hands and fingernails never evidenced the slightest hint of exposure to soap.

Wherever Hal made his daunting appearance at the Nit Picky Grade School, home of the Fighting Tomcats, the kids would "freeze" in their tracks. Then after a moment or two, they'd restart their halted actions. "Hateful" was his nickname.

"Hateful" Hal, it seemed, was quite proud of that label. He only had two friends that the kids knew of; he was one and the other was his overweight English Bulldog, Butch.

Butch could always be found waiting outside the school for his master. You didn't pet Butch! His spiked collar well suited his and Hal's dispositions. He and Butch were a good team. Hal boasted that petting his dog would result in needing a full hand replacement. No one challenged that boast. The **dog's odor** alone was enough to stifle one's temptation to go near him. Hal and Butch lived in South Nit Picky, across a railroad spur that led to Wicksburg. Most folks said that no one of any good ever came from South Nit Picky.

Hal didn't fair so well with teachers and grades, which resulted in his spending a great deal of time in the corner or at the desk in the hallway. What we didn't know then was that Hal was dyslexic. That meant he had an impossible time reading. However, in those days folks didn't know too much about that condition. Hal's promotions had simply been to pass on a difficult child. His parents didn't understand his learning problem either. They interpreted his behavior as laziness and orneriness, thus making his home life chaotic at times. But when it came to his dog Butch, it didn't make any difference to him whether his master Hal could read or not. As long as Hal fed, watered, and petted him, Butch was a loyal companion.

The Nit Picky kids stayed clear of Hal and Butch as much as possible. Often, when a person doesn't understand why others act as they do, they try to ignore them. It's easier to pretend they don't exist than to attempt to understand them. Children had made fun of Hal over his earlier years. He had been held back in school at least a couple of times, thus he had become older and bigger that most of his eighth-grade classmates. No one laughed at Hal anymore! He continually picked fights and acted tough and disrespectful. The Nit Picky gang had come to believe he was as cold as a new knife in the snow and twice as sharp. Most days he looked angrier than a cat cornered by a tub of soapy water. The only one Hal showed kindness to was his beloved Butch. Only Franny had noted that human side of Hal. Occasionally, he let down all pretenses around his pet. Franny had happened to see the sad loneliness in Hal's face that others had missed.

Valentine's Day was a few weeks away. Most of the Nit Picky kids loved that day of cards and parties, even the big eighth graders in Franny's class liked the excitement of the day. Over the years, Hal had grown to hate that day at school and would do most anything to miss it. He faked sickness so many years that his mother had finally caught on to his being sick every 14th of February. But why should he like the day, he never received any valentines. He hadn't for years. Oh, when he was younger he'd tried being a part of the merriment and had brought valentines, but having received few he'd quit trying.

At one Valentine's party, Hal became so angry that he threw a red cupcake across the room at the Valentine box. It missed the box and struck the sixth grade teacher, Mrs. Hilderbrand, on her backside. Hal got a paddling for that caper both at school and at home. He hated Valentines Day! Down deep he wanted friends, but his exterior repelled any hopes of that. He felt stupid in class, which added to his frustration.

It was their eighth-grade year when a crushing blow came to Hal that almost sent him over the edge. He was going home from school one day in January when a car slid on some ice and struck Butch. He didn't survive and Hal's heart nearly split in two. If sadness were water, Hal's would have filled an ocean. More than once, Franny caught Hal crying when he thought no one was around. With Butch gone, Hal felt totally alone. He was angry, sad, and even more withdrawn than any of the children had ever seen him. Most kids stayed even further away from him due to fear and indifference, but not Franny. She felt that underneath Hal's rough exterior there was a human being sinking further in the quicksand of life. He needed help.

Now a person can't solve everyone's problems and it's true that one must use caution in reaching out to help others, especially if they are complete strangers. However, the Lord can help a person to have wisdom in these matters. Franny sought that wisdom concerning Hal. She had been praying for him for some time and had tried to be pleasant to him whenever she had opportunity. She had read a Bible verse in Proverbs 3:27 "Do not withhold good from those who deserve it, when it is in your power to act." Franny knew that the Lord wanted her to help Hal if she was ever to teach him about Jesus' love and friendship.

Franny had noticed that Hal couldn't read very well. In fact, he didn't seem to be able to understand most written material. She also knew that Hal hadn't received valentines in the past. She had even been guilty of not fixing one for him, assuming he wouldn't want it anyway. But now she was seeing a different side of Hal and felt he had some problem that the teachers and his family were missing. Now that his dog was gone, Hal seemed more lost than ever and in need of a friend.

Franny found out that Hal's family was too poor to purchase another dog for him. She had an idea that she just knew was given her by the Lord. Franny had received some money for Christmas that she was saving for a new Easter dress. She figured that if she could convince some of the other Nit Picky gang to help, she could raise enough to purchase one of the English Bulldog pups advertised in the paper.

After some hard sell and charm with the gang, Franny reached her goal. Now, how would she give the gift to Hal? It was two days until the Valentines' party. Franny shared her plan with her parents, the kids, and Mrs. Playwright, their homeroom teacher. Principal Straightshooter was consulted concerning "Operation Bulldog", as Franny called it. Everything was set.

Valentine's Day came with its traditional cards, cup cakes, Red Hots, Hershey's Kisses wrapped in silver foil, love-me candy hearts, and ice cream. Hal sat off in the corner of the room looking more sad than mad. His mother had forced him to school that day. As usual, he knew that he wouldn't get any valentines, but then he hadn't brought any either. Even if he had wanted to, his parents couldn't have afforded them that year; his mother had been very poorly and had only recently returned to work at the school library. The party was nearly over when there was a rapid knock on their classroom door. Mrs. Playwright, pretending to be surprised, walked to the door. It was Principal Straightshooter. He was carrying a rather large square box wrapped in red and white paper. The valentine box was unusual in that it not only had a slot on its lid, but it was dotted with 1-inch holes evenly spaced around its upper edge. They looked like large polka dots.

144

The principal sat the mysterious box down directly in front of Hal and said, "Hal this special valentine was delivered to my office only moments ago. It's from your classmates. Franny organized it."

Hal, in a state of shock and disbelief, finally stammered out, "For m-e-e-e?"

"Yes," the class replied in unison, as if rehearsed.

At first, Hal didn't know what to say or do. He had only received a few valentines in his life and now, no doubt, he had a huge box full of them. Knowing that Hal couldn't read well, Franny had encouraged the Nit Picky gang to make valentine hearts with short sayings on them. They wrote things like, "Be Mine", "Happy Day", "Friend", "We Care", and "Surprise". Each had Hal's name on it and they were glued all over the large box. The red ribbon that Franny had placed around box had two words on it: "Happy Valentines". She knew that Hal could easily recognize that phrase.

Before Hal could really focus on the valentine hearts, the box "barked". Hal jerked back in surprise, the class laughed, and then he laughed too. With the kids urging, Hal quickly removed the lid on the box. Inside was a dark-eyed, fox-red English Bulldog male puppy with two white front feet and a white patch under its chin that was nearly heart shaped.

Tough-guy Hal felt tears welling up in his eyes as he lifted the excited, wiggling puppy from its temporary hiding place. Hal hugged the happy puppy that was licking his tear stained face. His mother and father, who had slipped in for the surprise, were drying their eyes, as the Nit Picky gang smiled with satisfaction.

Hal could only squeeze two words through his vocal cords, "Thank you". He didn't remember the last time he'd ever said those words. Hal knew that he had been given a valentine of love that he had never thought possible and he was grateful.

Hal received more than a puppy that day; with Franny's help, he acquired a new spiritual heart. He was also promised assistance with his reading problems. Franny had shared her observations of Hal's problem with Mr. Straightshooter. He, in turn, had been investigating some new findings concerning reading difficulties, that came to be known as dyslexia.

And what name did Hal give to his new dog? He chose it from the two words that Franny had written on the bow. He called his new buddy, "Valentine". And in time, "Valentine's" new owner received a new name too, "Happy", "Happy" Hal.

Chapter

31   The Jasper Place Mystery

The kids of Nit Picky, home of the Fighting Tomcats knew it as the "Snake House". Towns' folk called it "The Old Jasper Place". One could tell by the remaining gingerbread woodwork on its gables and porches that once it had been a beautiful house. The paintless columns and decaying shutters that hung precariously by only a nail or two gave other hints to its past stateliness. Nearly concealed by weeds and vines was the rusting iron fence that surrounded the desolate mansion. Many of the spear-type ornaments that once had adorned the iron pickets were missing, and sections of the fence were completely gone. Not one windowpane remained unbroken; most of them were totally gone. No one had lived in the "Jasper Place" for nearly forty years. Very little was remembered about the missing

Jaspers, except that they only had one child, Eric.

The town should have torn the deserted house down decades before, but money, politics, and perhaps fear of snakes had kept it haunting the corner of Third and Willow streets. To the neighbors the place was a disgrace, an eyesore, and a blemish to be cursed and "discursed". But to the Nit Picky gang it was a magnetic mystery that constantly tugged at their curiosity. Like an unopened surprise, it was a place of danger and intrigue waiting to be explored.

No doubt every kid in Nit Picky had heard the same parental warning: "Don't go near 'The Old Jasper Place', snakes will eat 'cha' alive."

One day, in an after school meeting of the Nit Picky gang at the "What-A-Burger", the topic of the "Jasper Place" surfaced again. "Tattling" Ted, Gerty's younger brother, began to talk seriously about exploring that spooky old house. Ted had only recently been allowed to rejoin the Nit Picky troop's activities.

"I want to know more about that place," Ted said with enthusiasm. "I hear that the Jasper's just up and moved out one night with only the shirts on their backs and were never heard from again." He continued, "Now if that's true, then there's bound to be some clues in that desolate house as to why they left so mysteriously. Maybe there are some treasures, too!" Ted exclaimed. "Besides," he said, "I've never seen a snake around that place." The truth was that he'd not seen a snake; he'd seen at least ten. "Tattling" Ted was like that about the truth; he didn't always tell it.

It didn't take too much to spark the Nit Picky gang's curiosity and Ted had peaked theirs. Even Franny wondered about the Jasper's mystery. The kids agreed that it was time the secrets shrouding the old Jasper Place should be revealed.

Phil announced, "Since the adults of Nit Picky haven't done anything to solve the 'Jasper Place' mysteries, then it's up to us kids."

The gang agreed that during the next weekend, while most folks would be uptown at the fall festival's gospel singing, they would explore the forlorn mansion.

It's important to understand something about "Tattling" Ted and his being out of the gang's circle for a time. Ted had a problem with his tongue. He told things on others, and talked too much about what folks did or didn't do or say. Sometimes he'd even make something up and tell it on others. He had caused lots of problems for some of the kids by "tattling" untruths. For example, Ted had told the story that Franny and Phil had been kissing under the fire escape during recess. He made sure their teacher heard him. Of course, it got back to their parents and had caused quite a ruckus. The truth was that Franny had been sitting in the shade of the fire escape as she helped Phil with his math. "Tattling" Ted had apologized to the kids and acted as if he had changed. Graciously, they had agreed to give him another chance, however most of the gang was still a bit dubious as to Ted's sincerity.

Saturday afternoon came and the gang gathered at the decaying mansion. Looking for snakes at every step, they very gingerly made their way across the broken back porch. They tugged the back door open making a harsh creaking sound, then it crashed to the floor in a cloud of dust. The gang screamed in chorus! Regaining their composure, they eased inside the eerie house. Their every step made a resounding "er-er-re-re-ak". But still no snakes.

The vacated house was full of cobwebs, decaying furniture, broken glass, peeling wall paper, ruined wall hangings, and fallen plaster, but still no snakes. Using their flashlights, the kids made their way up the rickety staircase to the bedrooms. The smell of the musty, molded old house was stifling; Franny sneezed fifteen times in a row sending echoes throughout the ghastly structure. But still no snakes.

Arriving at the top step, they moved cautiously across warped flooring to a room that appeared to have belonged to the Jaspers's son. The name Eric was still faintly visible on the ravished door. Easing in, they found his room amazingly in tact, except, of course, for the many years of neglect. The gang began to search the drawers and closets for clues and treasures. But still no snakes.

While digging through the dingy junk, Ted shouted, "I've found something!"

It was a diary, Eric's diary. Trying to get more light for reading, the kids gathered on the dusty old bed near a broken window. Carefully they opened the aged book and began to read. At first it was pretty boring stuff, but after about twenty pages they began to have their questions answered.

It seemed that Eric was a typical boy who loved the out-of-doors. He was fascinated with fishing, and collecting frogs, spiders and, yes, snakes. On one entry Eric wrote that near the town creek, just below "THE HILL", he had found a snake. It was a couple feet long and copper in color. Capturing it, he had brought it home in a cage-like device that he always took on his "expeditions," as he called them.

"Snakes were against the house rules," he wrote in his diary, "but a little lie to Father and Mother wouldn't hurt." He didn't show them the snake, of course, but he had told them that the covered cage was a secret project for science class. He wrote in his diary that he had become quite sneaky at telling lies.

With each page of the diary, the gang became more engrossed in this Nit Picky kid of years gone by. He gave a day by day account of his new pet snake. On day five, he told that from reading about snakes he realized that he had captured a female copperhead; he was glad that he had been so careful.

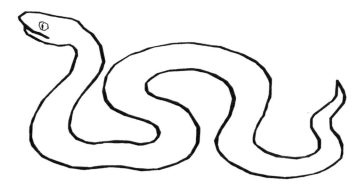

"One bite and I could have been a goner," he wrote. "Father and Mother would kill me if they knew what I was keeping in my closet."

On day thirteen with the snake, tragedy happened. When Eric came home from school, the snake was gone. She had managed to spread the wire netting enough to slither through.

The gang looked away from the diary, then at each other. Then, as if practiced, they exclaimed in unison, "A copperhead!" With the same unity, their heads all disappeared over the sides of the bed as their eyes peered under it for a look-see, but still no snakes. "Whew!" they sighed.

They read on. Eric wrote that things went okay for a few weeks, with no sight of "Miss Copper", as he had named her. Reading on hurriedly, the gang found that that was soon to change. Mother was first to spot a snake in the basement wash room. It was small, and Eric knew it wasn't "Miss Copper"; he began to panic. He realized that "Miss Copper's" extra round middle must have been full of eggs. She had escaped to nest and hatch her young. Now her young "coppers" were on the move. Eric wrote that his lies increased to hide his knowledge about the snakes. His father was bitten by one of the small snakes and became quite ill for several days. Eric was near dying himself with guilt. He couldn't sleep at night for fear of the snakes and of Father. No one else in his fine house rested either. They left lights on and wore heavy boots. They checked every drawer and closet for snakes. Each new scream that echoed throughout the house announced another snake.

Saturday, February 11, 1922: "Dear Diary, Father hired a fellow to come to the house today to chase the snakes out with smoke, but he ended up setting the basement on fire; it did a lot of damage. Father fired the man on the spot; as yet another snake slithered across Father's boot. The fellow left quickly without a fuss or money and seemed quite happy to do so."

The gang's saucer-sized eyeballs began to peer around the darkening room. Knowing that they should leave before night came, they remained huddled on that old bed straining to read in the fading daylight.

Tuesday, April 13, 1922: "Dear Diary, This is my last entry to you. Father told me that tonight we're leaving this house with nothing but the clothes on our backs. So I must leave even you behind. Father is acting crazed over the snakes. The snakes have multiplied to the point that no one can live here. Father said that for us to stay longer would mean insanity or death or both. All efforts to rid the house of the snakes have failed. All hope is gone. I'm not sure where we are going. Father exclaimed that Nit Picky would only see the dust from our tires. Just think, Diary, all I did was bring home one little snake. Now look what has happened. If my father ever learns that it was me who caused this chaos, it would be better for me to have died here with the snakes. For one to read this diary means you've entered the house. Beware of the snakes!" It was signed, "Eric Jasper, age twelve and afraid that I'll never see thirteen."

The old bed shook with scared kids as they realized that it had gotten dark outside and that their flashlights were fading out. Walking as one body, the gang made their way to the stairs; wedging in its entrance they saw that they'd have to separate in order to maneuver the steps. "Tattling" Ted grasped the railing with whitened knuckles. He was sorry that he had suggested this adventure. Yet they hadn't seen any snakes and, after all, Ted reasoned, they had found the diary.

As the gang crossed the living room remains, they discovered results of the fire, mentioned in the diary. Weakened by fire and time, some of the floor gave way and Ted fell through. He would have crashed to the basement except for his out stretched arms. He tightly grasped the diary in his right hand as the broken flooring slapped the basement floor. The gang froze in their tracks. Slowly they directed their remaining light towards Ted and the new opening he'd made. Ted yelled! The gang grabbed his arms. Then Franny screamed! "Snakes!" The basement was full of snakes. "Tattling" Ted looked down and fainted. The splintered flooring kept him from being pulled up, but letting go of him would allow him to slip into the mass of snakes. The vipers, doing their best to strike Ted's heels, crawled and hissed only a few feet below his dangling body. With the gang shaking, crying, screaming, and blaming each other for their being in such a mess, the last flicker of flashlight faded out. Franny prayed, they all prayed! Just then the kids heard sirens and saw flashing red lights streaming through the missing windows and bouncing off the walls. Ted woke up.

People were yelling, "Anyone in there?" It was the Nit Picky police, fire department and some frightened parents. A neighbor had spotted flashlights in the "Old Jasper Place" and had called the police. Word had spread quickly in Nit Picky. But then, it always did.

"Yes!" yelled the kids. "Help us! There are snakes in here, and Ted is trapped! Help, please help!"

Quickly, but carefully, the rescuers made their way toward the stranded kids; but more of the floor began to give way so they had to go out and come in the back door. With saws, axes, and the use of a ladder for Ted to wrap his arms around, the kids were taken out of the crumbling room one by one. The hissing snakes seemed disappointed that Ted hadn't joined them for "dinner". The firemen used some torches to discourage the snakes that had begun to make their way up to the first floor. Safely outside, the kids were so relieved that even the lecture they received was mild compared to what they had just been through. Resembling a ghost, Ted still clutched Eric's diary.

The following Monday, as the gang met in the school lunchroom, they were eager to share with others their harrowing adventure. But it was "Tattling" Ted who made the most dramatic revelation. Unable to sleep much over the weekend, he had re-read Eric's diary. Then he'd read some Bible verses that Franny had given to him some weeks before in her effort to help him see his "tongue problem". In his reading, Ted realized that he and Eric were much alike; they both had disobeyed the rules and hurt others. But, unlike Eric who had let a snake loose, Ted knew that he had let hurtful words loose.

"Too often," Ted said, "my words have been cruel, untrue, or stretched to fit my desire. Like Eric's snakes, my words multiplied, got out of control, and couldn't be recaptured." Going on, Ted added, "One of the scriptures that Franny gave me was Romans 3:13-14; that says in part, '...their tongues practice deceit. The poison of vipers is on their lips.' I realize now how the deceitful, poisonous words on my lips have been harmful; much like the snakes' poison in the 'Jasper Place.' I'm very sorry for being 'Tattling' Ted and I've learned my lesson."

That time, with Christ's help, Ted did change his ways. He kept the diary; it would be a reminder of his lesson. It was the only thing saved from that horrible place. The house with its snakes was soon burned and bulldozed over. By the following summer, a beautified little park occupied that corner. But the Nit Picky gang never forgot the 'Jasper Place', especially Ted.

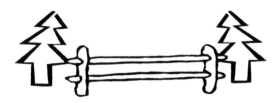

Chapter

32　The Day Concludes

The air chilled with the approaching evening, as the "Aged Storyteller's" mind returned from his childhood days in Nit Picky. He read once again the etched writing on the weathered stone atop cemetery hill.

"Here lies Franny Goodman
Born September 1, 1948-Died December 25, 1968
Her life was short, yet full, she was a true friend and
a real beauty to all."

He remembered one of her favorite scriptures: "Be wise in the way you act toward outsiders; make the **most of every opportunity.**" (Col. 4:5) Franny had truly lived that verse.

Gently he raised the chrome-plated kickstand of his customized blue-Schwinn bike and pointed it toward the crest of "THE HILL". This time however, with the blacktop in place of the old gravel road and his years of cross-country riding, the spry "Storyteller" sailed down the hill, across the bridge, and past the boarded-up high school. As the wind whistled across his older, but still-keen ears, he knew in his heart that he heard the spirit of Franny's laughter and approving applause.

Her voice, as sweet as so many years ago, whispered, "You always were a 'real man' to me; you just had to find out for yourself. Don't forget that Jesus always loves you and so do I."

A smile formed on the face of "Clutts" Clinkmyer, our "Storyteller", as the memories of Franny and the gang lingered in his heart. While coasting by the vacant lot where the Nit Picky Grade School, home of the Fighting Tomcats, had once stood, he

155

softly prayed, "Thanks, Lord, for Franny; what she was to all of us, may we always be to others."

The day ended, but who knows what memories still lodge in the "Aged Storyteller's" heart?

<u>Indexes</u>

Chapter-Title	Lessons
01-New Kid in Town	Humility (look past flaws)
02-Hidden Pain	Forgiveness
03-The Bully	Turning other cheek
04-Tight Pants	Pride
05-Too Much Cooked Goose	Evil tongue
06-Nit Picky Goes to Chicago	Need for others
07-Cemetery Hill	Worth/Christ's love
08-The Big Race	Brotherly love/sacrifice
09-A New Start	Unselfishness
10-The Christmas Flute	Jealousy/repentance
11-Rich Boy	Selfishness
12-Strange Request	Faithful in small things
13-Town by the Spring	Pettiness/divisions
14-You Hafta Spit on the Bait	Kindness
15-The Camping Trip	Witness/care for others
16-Sad Day in Nit Picky	Change/adjustments
17-Mayhem at the City Dump	Hell
18-"Greedy" Gerty	Greed
19-Odor in Nit Picky	Personal hygiene
20-Nit Picky's Secret Room	Treasures/priorities
21-The Lost Ring	Gossip
22-"Sneaky's" New Home	Cheating/honesty
23-Unbelievable	Lying
24-Confusion in Nit Picky	Clear communication
25-"Devil Lady"	Judging others
26-Nit Picky's Big Party	Bitterness/anger
27-The Cliff	Procrastination
28-Letter from Texas	Bigotry
29-The Life that was Missed	Spiritual blindness
30-A Valentine for Hal	Good deeds
31-The Jasper Place Mystery	Poisonous tongue
32-The Day Concludes	Redeem the time

Chapter-Title	Scripture Reference
01-New Kid in Town	Eph.4:2
02-Hidden Pain	Col.3:12-14
03-The Bully	Mt.5:39/1Co.13:4-5
04-Tight Pants	Pr.16:18/Luke 14:11
05-Too Much Cooked Goose	James 3:5-6
06-Nit Picky Goes to Chicago	Rom.12:4-5
07-Cemetery Hill	Eph.2:4-5
08-The Big Race	Ecc.11:1/Ro.12:10
09-A New Start	Eph.4:32/Ro.12:20
10-The Christmas Flute	1Co.3:3/Mt.5:23-24
11-Rich Boy	Luke 6:38
12-Strange Request	Luke 19:17
13-Town by the Spring	Mt.23:24
14-You Hafta Spit on the Bait	1Th.5:15
15-The Camping Trip	Mt.5:16
16-Sad Day in Nit Picky	Dt.34:9a
17-Mayhem at the City Dump	Rev.20:10
18-"Greedy" Gerty	Luke 12:15/Gal.6:7
19-Odor in Nit Picky	Mt.7:24-27
20-Nit Picky's Secret Room	Mt.6:19-21
21-The Lost Ring	Lev.19:16
22-"Sneaky's" New Home	Ro.12:3/Ex.20:15
23-Unbelievable	Lev.19:11b
24-Confusion in Nit Picky	Pr.4:23
25-"Devil Lady"	1Sa.16:7
26-Nit Picky's Big Party	Eph.4:31-32
27-The Cliff	Ecc.12:1
28-Letter from Texas	Gal.3:28
29-The Life that was Missed	Dt.29:4
30-A Valentine for Hal	Pr.3:27
31-The Jasper Place Mystery	Ro.3:13-14
32-The Day Concludes	Col. 4:5

159

Chapter-Title	Special Days
01-New Kid in Town	School Start
05-Too Much Cooked Goose	Easter
09-A New Start	Thanksgiving
10-The Christmas Flute	Christmas
15-The Camping Trip	Labor Day Weekend
18-"Greedy" Gerty	Easter
21-The Lost Ring	Christmas
26-Nit Picky's Big Party	End of school
29-The Life that was Missed	Christmas
30-A Valentine for Hal	Valentine's Day

About the Author

Kenneth L. Clark was born in Paducah, Kentucky but grew up in Mounds, Illinois, near Cairo, to the parents of Arthur and Irma Clark. He has been an Illinois pastor for the last twenty-five years. Prior to his call into the pastoral ministry, Kenneth taught high school in Greenup, Illinois and worked as a draftsperson for Marathon Oil Pipe Line Company near Casey, IL. He graduated from Eastern Illinois University and has taken seminary classes and additional classes in pastoral care, speech, writing, and computer. He has written several articles for newsletters, the *Illinois Baptist* State paper, and a local paper in McLeansboro, IL. Besides his love of writing, and the dramatic storytelling of his Nit Picky episodes, he enjoys music, drama, landscaping, woodworking, fishing, and camping.

Clark is married to Mary Sue (Hardway). They have two grown daughters: Anita, a nurse, and Valerie, a schoolteacher, and one grand daughter Michaela Lucas.

Order Information

Additional copies of this book are
available by mail order.

Please send $15.20 to:
($11.95 per book + $3.25 shipping)
Shipping is paid on orders
of 12 or more books.

Kenneth L. Clark
2301 Jerome Lane
Cahokia, Illinois 62206-2601

For questions, write or e-mail:
mary_suec@hotmail.com